JOURNEY'S END

Women's Fiction Historical Saga of the Oregon Territory

OREGON AT LAST
BOOK 1

A.T. BUTLER

CHAPTER ONE

Caroline Harper tucked her small hand into the large, rough hand of Daniel Mills. Taking a deep, steadying breath, she looked out over the side of the mountain. They were walking down the trail into the Willamette Valley and the Oregon Territory, after more than six months of daily striving to get here. It had taken so much for her to get to this point, to be taking these final steps at the end of her long journey. Hers was now a rougher, tanner, much more worn hand than she had had when she left New York City nearly a year earlier. In the city, that hand had at every moment been protected by kid gloves. Never had it needed to learn how to bake biscuits over a campfire, haul buckets of water, or drive a two-thousand-pound ox over uneven terrain.

Caroline's hand was no longer soft and white and coddled.

Now it was much stronger, much more capable.

Now, after six months on the Oregon Trail, and more

time traveling west before that, Caroline had hands that could cook. Her hands could shoot and take care of herself in ways that she'd never had cause to in her previous life in the city.

And these were the hands that tall, handsome Daniel Mills raised to his lips to kiss tenderly as they followed the trail.

"Well, now, Miss Harper," he said with mock solemnity. "What do you plan to do with the rest of your day?"

She laughed, light-hearted for the first time in ever so long. "I think we have a bit of walking to do yet, before I have a minute of free time to choose something else. Will we be making camp on the mountain again tonight?"

"I don't think so. The trail going down isn't nearly as winding as it was coming up the eastern side, and the teams can go much faster downhill than they could lugging the wagons uphill. It might be a long day, but I think my father intends for us all to make camp in the valley tonight."

"Your father," she breathed, her voice full of admiration. "Leading this wagon company all by himself for the last few weeks after William Sullivan died. I don't know how he managed. You must be so proud of him."

"He might not have managed if so many people hadn't pitched in. George Mills is a lot of things, but he's not invincible. The Findleys and Pastor Montgomery and my mother—"

"And you."

Daniel nodded, acknowledging. "And me. And plenty of others. Everyone doing their part. Just like all the folks that have been helping you since you were left alone," he added gently.

"After John died . . ."

Caroline swallowed down tears that had welled up unbidden. After her older brother had fallen to his death at the Snake River, she had been left to make her way to the Oregon Territory completely on her own. Though she never would have asked for help, she had been shocked when she realized how many people were there to offer it, that no one expected her to manage without it.

The Sullivan–Mills wagon company was made up of around fifty wagons, about forty families. They had come from all over the country, gathering in the last proper town on the frontier. The company had left Independence, Missouri, at the end of April and spent the previous six months walking, riding, and desperately striding westward to the Oregon Territory.

"After John died," she said again, "that's when I finally realized what you all have meant to me. I couldn't do any of this without you. Or Hannah."

"And you won't have to," Daniel assured her with a smile. "My sister, Abby, wants to make friends with you, by the way. You might find her inviting herself to a social outing or two with you and Hannah."

"Social?" Caroline laughed. "After so long of just barely surviving, I can't even imagine it."

"Mark my words. We might still be sleeping in wagons tonight, but you just watch. Within weeks, folks will have walls up, floors down, roofs over our heads. The hardest part might be patience, with everyone ready to be home as soon as possible, but I'm sure my pa has a plan. He'll make sure the whole wagon company is settled in for the winter, maybe even before he worries about settling in himself."

"And us?" Caroline asked tentatively. "Will you and I . . . ?" She blushed, needing to know but petrified to put it into words.

"We," Daniel said emphatically. "You and I. The future Mr. and Mrs. Daniel Mills will also be settled in a home together. Before winter hits. I promise."

"You promise," she said breathlessly.

"I told you I was going to love you until the day I die, Caroline Harper," he teased her. "Those aren't just words. That means I am going to make sure you have food, and a roof, and a new pretty dress whenever you want it. You know that, don't you?"

"I do. And I'm so grateful for you."

"I just don't know exactly when yet."

"Since we're still actually *on* the trail to Oregon?" She gestured to the covered wagons and oxen walking down the mountain in front of them.

He chuckled. "Yes, since we're still actually on the trail," he agreed. "That reminds me. I promised Pa I would scout ahead today, find us a place to camp for the night. Will you be all right if I leave you?"

"Of course. Hannah is back there somewhere." She gestured over her shoulder. "I'll be just fine. I know you will take care of us. Daniel, I have never felt more safe than I do with you."

"Good." He grinned. "And sometime in the next day or two you and I will sit down together and make an actual plan for an actual wedding."

"And an actual home."

"With an actual kitchen."

"Where I suppose I will have to make actual supper, won't I?"

Daniel laughed again. "I know you haven't been doing it long, but I guarantee you're a better cook than I am."

She smiled up at him and squeezed his hand. "As long as it's for you, I'm happy to cook."

"Do you want me to walk you to the Sullivans' wagon?"

"No, you go ahead. I'll find Hannah in a moment."

He kissed her cheek, hurriedly and impulsively, before he dashed off down the trail, around the Valentine wagon that was just ahead of them, to the very front of the caravan where his father, Captain Mills, led the company.

Caroline was alone again, but for maybe the first time since she had been forced to leave her home in New York City the previous fall, she did not feel lonely. The last year had been the most difficult of her life—leaving the home she had grown up in and the life she had been promised, forced to trek west to an unknown future, through hunger and Indian attacks and broken wagon axles. But it had also been the most rewarding experience of her life. The Caroline Harper who walked down the mountain into the Willamette Valley was a very different Caroline Harper than had walked down the cobblestone streets of the eastern metropolis.

She wouldn't have it any other way.

Looking around at the wagon company progressing all around her, Caroline realized that she was several wagon-lengths ahead of her best friend, and the family with which she had made her home since her brother died. She slowed her steps, letting the two Sullivan wagons catch up to her as she stayed out of the way of all the animals and wagons that passed.

"Where's your beau?" Junior Sullivan asked with a grin when he saw her.

The oldest boy—and now only male—of the Sullivan family drove their lead wagon, in which the family slept each night. The huge, two-thousand-pound oxen at his side seemed downright eager to be heading down the trail.

"Where's your sister?" she returned, ignoring his question.

He indicated with a nod over his shoulder. "Back there. She's driving the other wagon at the moment. I'm sure she wants some company if Mills has deserted you."

"Junior," Caroline said with a shake of her head. That sixteen-year-old boy was gaining confidence every day the family's responsibilities rested on his shoulders. Now he treated her exactly the way he did his own sisters—teasing and vexing. "You be careful, or I will tell Daniel that you're speaking ill of him," she joked in return.

He only grinned and tipped his hat as he led his wagon past her.

His older sister and Caroline's best friend, Hannah Sullivan, was only steps behind that wagon, leading her own team of enormous oxen that pulled the family's supply wagon. This far in the journey it was significantly more empty than it had been when they left Missouri. The family had practically run out of food only a couple days prior. It still held clothes and some furniture, but the Sullivans had considered abandoning the second wagon altogether at least once.

"Did Daniel desert you?" Hannah asked when she spotted Caroline.

"You sound just like your brother." She fell into step alongside the trail. "You know perfectly well he is very busy and important, and his father can't possibly function without him."

"And that's one of the reasons you love him," Hannah prodded.

Caroline blushed. That word—love. It was so strong, so new, that actually saying it out loud still overwhelmed her.

"Yes, but . . . maybe I'm just impatient. I know he wants to marry me, and I know he wants to take care of me, but there's so much else claiming his time that I worry when he'll manage to do it all."

"Do you really think Daniel Mills is not going to make building you a home his first priority? Do you know him at all?" Hannah laughed. "Caroline Harper, you have been the only thing on his mind for the last thousand miles at least."

"You're right. I know you're right. I'm just . . . I'm so happy, and I'm so afraid that I'll lose it all."

"You won't lose it all. I promise," Hannah said, serious now that she saw her friend's vulnerability. "It might not be tomorrow, but Daniel Mills is going to marry you and make a home with you somewhere you can be safe for the rest of your life."

"And until he does?"

"Until he does, you have a home with the Sullivans, silly. Just as you always have. You come with us, Caroline," Hannah said, linking her free arm through her friend's. "We've been together for six months already. I'm not ready to let you go off on your own just yet."

CHAPTER TWO

It took all day to get there—just as Daniel had predicted
—but the Sullivan–Mills wagon company made camp
that evening just after sunset at the bottom of the
mountain that lay in the eastern section of the Oregon
Territory. It was a long day, but at least it was the last.
Even where they ended up making camp, the ground was
still at a bit of a slope, but each and every one of the
migrants told themselves they had made it to the
Willamette Valley, finally, after all the doubt and stress of
the previous months.

"Caroline, I can't believe it! Can you believe it? I
can't believe it."

Hannah threw her arms around Caroline, wrapping
her in a hug, utterly heedless to the dirt and sweat that
coated them both after their long day. The pair sat on
the wagon seat of one of the Sullivans' wagons, in an
effort to be higher to see across the landscape. The sun
had already sunk below the western horizon, but now
that they were finally in the Oregon Territory, the lights

of homes and campfires scattered across the countryside glowed in the twilight.

"We're finally at the foot of the mountain, on the Oregon Trail, with all the Willamette Valley stretching out before us. We've been aiming for this place for months, and now we're actually here," Caroline answered with a laugh. "I have had a blister on my right foot since Fort Boise. I'm wearing a bonnet that you yourself gave me months ago, and I'm not sure the bruises on my legs from hauling water buckets have fully healed in months. We've been through so much, Hannah. When will you believe it?"

The view from this vantage revealed a lush, green countryside of rolling hills, wide meadows, and thick stands of trees. Though Caroline didn't know a thing about farming, she could see enough to understand why so many men and women had looked to this territory as a promised land of sorts. There seemed to be so much opportunity just in being here.

"Oh, we'll see. Maybe sometime next year. After we've lived all four seasons here, perhaps. You never know. It could be a *very* vivid dream, blisters and all."

"Very," she agreed. "Do you want me to pinch you to wake you up?"

Hannah grinned and nudged her gently. "You know what I mean, don't you? I've spent so long thinking about being here that now . . . well, it's just something I have got to get used to, I suppose."

"You will. Sooner than you think, I'll bet. Especially if Ben has anything to say about it. Has he spoken to you about his plans yet?"

Hannah shook her head. "He's just as tied up with

making sure the whole community is settled as Daniel is, it seems. But I know Ma needs me more than I need to be a wife, so I'm content to wait."

"Will he settle near your family if you ask him to?"

Hannah grinned. "He already offered."

"I'm so happy for you," Caroline said sincerely.

"I'm happy for *us*," Hannah corrected her. "We have both reached the end of the trail in a far different situation than when we started. What with my brother and father . . ." She trailed off, composed herself, and cleared her throat. "With losing members of *both* of our families, and both meeting our future husbands, we couldn't possibly have predicted how different everything is now. I know I keep saying this, but I still can't believe it."

Caroline squeezed her hand and looked out over the dirty white canvas tops that housed all their friends. Her friend was right—she never would have guessed what this would feel like when she had first been torn away from New York.

"Come," said Hannah, climbing down from the wagon. "We should help Ma with supper."

"Only a few more nights eating over a campfire," Caroline added excitedly.

"Let's hope."

The two young women helped Mrs. Sullivan with supper, and with readying the smaller Sullivan children, Patience and Martha, for bedtime. They had been living out of these wagons for so long that one more night—or three, or even five—couldn't make much difference, but the thrum of excitement that rolled through the camp was almost palpable. Each of the emigrant families knew that they were in the final stretch before making their long-term home.

With such excitement urging them on, the next several days flew by. Each hour was packed full with preparations for establishing their more permanent settlement. Captain Mills called numerous meetings and votes of the families that he had led across the continent, aiming to unite the community and establish their place in the new territory as quickly as he could. Now that everyone was safely in the Oregon Territory, there was no longer a need to stick so closely together if they didn't want. Some of the families—the Owens family and one of the Waters brothers, for example—left the camp within days to make their own ways. The town of Dempsey had been recently established, and they sought to join that more settled community.

Most, however, stuck close to Captain Mills and the neighbors they had formed close friendships with over the previous months. There was a safety and comfort there that they were loath to give up. The community that they had built over the months traveling from Independence was familiar and dependable. And so, they all pitched in, working together to get settled before the first snow in a couple months.

One night, almost a week into their time in Oregon, Daniel returned from a long day of scouting and joined Caroline with the Sullivans just before supper.

"There's a few choice spots not far from here," he said. He placed the gift of a bag full of rice near Mrs. Sullivan's feet. "With all the fresh water and arable land, there's not really a wrong choice for where to settle this group. A few of the local men from Dempsey—"

"The ones who rescued us?" Martha asked.

Daniel nodded to the little girl. "Precisely. Their town of Dempsey is a short ride away from here, couple hours maybe, so they're all well familiar with the soil and the resources of this part of the territory. A few of them, the ones without wives and families back home, have stuck around to offer my father more help and advice when he needs it. And they think we should settle near where some of the tributaries flow out of the mountains before they reach the Sandy River."

"How far is that from here?" Caroline asked.

"Less than a day. If the men of this company vote to make that change, we can pull up stakes the next morning and be settled again by the afternoon."

"And then what?" Junior asked.

"Then we dig in. I imagine there's an efficient way to go about it, laying out the proposed lots and roads, making sure that each man has enough labor for what he needs done, those kinds of things. Pa is taking it one step at a time, I think. Since there's so much to consider."

"What will we name the new town?" Patience asked.

"Sullivanville!" Junior shouted with a laugh.

"I'm sure there will be a vote for the name too," Daniel said.

Hannah grinned. "We're very fond of democracy in this country."

"If you all have ideas, I'm happy to share them with the other men. And, Mrs. Sullivan, I am happy to vote for your family by proxy if you'd like. My father knows fully well how much your family has done for this community, even if there's no male head of the household to vote. This will be something we all have to live with for a long time, so don't be shy." He stood again, replacing his hat on his head. "Mama will be expecting me for supper, but I wanted to bring that rice for you all first."

Caroline stood with him, anxious for a moment alone together.

She wanted to ask Daniel about his plans for them, for their home and life and wedding. It hadn't even been a week since he'd reassured her, but she had barely seen him in that time, and so many other decisions were being made by everyone else around them. She knew she was welcome to live with the Sullivans as long as she needed; she would always have a home with them. But Caroline was more than ready to put her own roots down, to begin her life as a wife. She could not do so, however, without her husband. And he was too busy scouting for his father to be able to give her the attention and assurances she so craved.

He caught her eye as he stepped away, and she joined him.

"Thank you for the rice," she began, "and for staying to talk to us. I've missed you."

"I've missed you too," he said, looking down into her eyes. "I'm sorry I can't see you more. There's just so much to be done."

She nodded in understanding, swallowing down her protests.

"Soon, once we're settled for the long term, I promise that you and I will have a special day. Or maybe an afternoon. Just the two of us."

"You promise? I'm sorry I keep questioning. I'm just so anxious to be settled."

"I promise. Believe me that I would much rather go on a walk with you than try again to convince old Tom Jameson that the general store is not a priority before homes are." He brought her hand to his mouth and kissed the worn palm. "I just need a little more time to help my father get everything settled. And then I'm all yours."

"I understand. Thank you."

He tipped his hat to her, gently let go of her hand, and disappeared into the night toward where the Mills family was camped.

Just as Daniel had predicted, the following evening the men of the community gathered to discuss the options available to them and vote on the next steps. Most of the men looked to Captain Mills for leadership, but he knew better than to insist on his own will.

The decision was made as a group, and the wagon company—now the new Oregon settlers—pulled up their camp early one morning and fell into the same easy routine, the same straight caravan of wagons, trekking toward the river where the leaders had determined would be the best place to settle. A long, cool river wound through the rolling hills, wide and slow in some stretches and narrower in others, from where it origi-nated in the mountains through to the west where it emptied into the ocean some hundred miles away. The company would be settling on either side of one of the narrow pieces of the river.

The main street of the new town—whatever it would

be named—would live on the north side of the river, while secondary public buildings would have designated sites on the south side. A bridge wide enough for wagons would be built before anything else, to promote easy settling before the weather grew too cold. Families wishing to farm could claim their acres of land on either side, while the plans for roads in between such settlements would be a community project. To hear Daniel talk about it, it seemed as though Captain Mills had been planning this town since long before they reached it, and it was only a matter of time before it would all reach fruition.

CHAPTER THREE

After months of traveling, they were almost there. The choice for the new settlement's location had been made for the good of all, by popular vote by the adult men in the wagon company. It was finally time for one last push toward their new home.

First thing in the morning after the vote, the company of emigrants left their camp at the foot of the mountains and spent one last day traveling. It would take the wagons the better part of seven hours to reach the spot on the river that had been chosen, but then they would be done. The exhausted men and women who had toiled for months to get this far west could finally stop. The worn-out animals could finally rest. They would never have to move again if they didn't want to.

Though she had to trudge through a long morning of helping Hannah drive one of the Sullivan wagons, Caroline was ebullient when they finally reached their destination. Though still living out of wagons, at least they were able to make camp before sunset. The chances to do so had been few and far between when they had been traveling west on the trail. She would need to get used to life in one place again.

As she helped Hannah and Junior with the Sullivans' animals, Caroline took a cautious look around. This place right here would be where she would, after all this time, make a home. This would be the view that she took in each and every day.

Enormous, thick stands of pine trees extended in every direction, tall enough to obstruct her view of parts of the river and the mountains beyond. This seemingly inexhaustible supply of lumber would be cleared to make room for the town, while at the same time offering the materials that would create the very walls and roofs to go over their heads. Though it was midafternoon, the warmest part of the day, the sky above the pines was thick with gray clouds that constantly threatened rain but had yet to provide any.

When Caroline returned to the family's camp with two buckets of water for the oxen, she found Hannah cuddled close to Benjamin Findley, both leaning against the side of the Sullivans' sleeping wagon.

"Don't let me interrupt," Caroline called out, ostentatiously avoiding looking at her friend. "Don't mind me!"

"Don't be a goose," Hannah teased, hurrying to take one of the buckets from her. "Ben was just telling me about all the places nearby we can choose from to settle more permanently."

"Tomorrow I'll take your mother and Junior," he added. "You too if you'd like. Captain Mills wants to make sure each family is happily settled and has at least a plan before the end of the week. He says he wants to head off any strife or disagreement before it happens and have everything in hand by the time a government surveyor can come out. Probably in the spring."

"Does he expect disagreement?" Caroline asked. It had seemed to her that most, if not all, the folks in the wagon company had been agreeable and easy to keep the peace with.

"It's hard to say. There's a lot of men who have been forced to the very edge of what they can bear, and now that they have got more food in their bellies and solid ground under their feet, it might be easier for them to find things to complain about. Exhaustion puts folks on edge."

"Well, that doesn't seem right," Hannah said.

Ben shrugged. "It's hard to predict what someone might do when they're afraid of losing the little bit of security they finally managed to grasp. But, you know, it might not be anything anyway. Tomorrow we'll go out into the surrounding farmland and stake a claim for the Sullivans. Everything will be squared away. You'll see."

Caroline busied herself with the oxen again, so Hannah and her beloved could say their goodbyes in peace. Internally, however, she was in turmoil. Would Daniel also be going to find their home? Would she be included in any of the decisions, or would she constantly be wondering what was being done on her behalf?

Though she felt stuck and unsure of what she could do next, Caroline never rested. There was plenty to do to build this new life in one place, plenty to keep her busy even without walking so many miles every day.

Even so, after the company began to build their home on the broad tract of land on either side of the river, Caroline actually found time to read again, though she hadn't in months. She couldn't fell trees like the men, and she didn't have children to look after like some of the women. There were tasks everywhere that needed to be done, but none of them came natural to Caroline. She couldn't even help provide food for the table like Junior with his hunting or Faith Waters with her foraging.

Hannah tried to encourage Caroline, but the former New York socialite struggled to find her place in a town that wasn't quite a town, in a home that was really just a wagon, with a fiancé who didn't seem to have time for her.

Three nights after they had made a more permanent camp, George Mills—he no longer wanted to be called Captain—set the time and place for the final vote on the new community's name. Furthermore, he had visited the households that did not have men leading them—the Hudsons, the Sullivans, the Buchanans—to get feedback from the families who would not otherwise get a vote.

Hannah and Junior had made a private bet between the two of them about what the town would be called, though their mother tried to talk them out of gambling with anything too valuable. Caroline vowed to stay out of it.

The meeting was to be just after sunset, next to the lone, impossibly tall ponderosa pine tree that towered above all others. Already that tree had been singled out as a landmark of significance, and now, as the site of the founding of whatever the town was to be named, it was even more so.

Caroline had finished washing dishes after supper, and was now pacing around the edge of the Sullivans' campsite watching as the men streamed toward the pine tree in pairs and trios. Finally, the man she had been watching for broke away from his own camp and began walking with the others. She caught up to him as he strode across the meadow toward the huddle of men around the campfire in the distance.

"Daniel!"

He paused at the sound of his name, and visibly relaxed when he saw who had called him.

"The most beautiful girl in Oregon," he called out to her, offering his hands. "To what do I owe the pleasure?"

"I had an idea for the town name," Caroline said. "If it's not too late."

"No, I can still add to the list. What did you have in mind?"

"I thought maybe something that spoke to the . . . well, the *paradise* that we've found ourselves in." She looked around at the green, verdant rolling hills, and at the evergreens that towered over them in a seemingly protective embrace. "Maybe something with the word *Eden?*"

"Our own land of milk and honey. I love it. And I bet if no one else, I can get Pastor Montgomery to vote that way too."

"Well, you know, vote for whatever you think best, of course. It was just an idea."

"And it is a brilliant one."

"When will we be told of the results?"

"It is to be a private vote, so I believe Pa will take a day to count all the votes so he can announce it as soon as he can. He thought it might be a festive occasion for everyone, including the little ones who might be in bed already."

Caroline smiled. "That sounds lovely."

"I gotta admit, I'm beat. I'll be glad for one extra day before things start up again."

"You've been busy for your father?" she prompted.

"Very. I know Ben filled you girls in a little on what Pa wants us to do, but even I didn't realize how exhausting it would be. There are just so many families, and everyone has a strong opinion. This is a gorgeous country with acres and acres of lush land, but even still, it only goes so far. Pa's trying to balance a million different concerns. I'm glad I don't have his job."

"And have you looked into where our home will be yet? I'd love to hear about it."

"Caro, I promise when I know, you'll know." He frowned, looking down into her face with concern. "It seems like every time we talk it's the same worry."

"It's just hard for me to have to wait and not be able to *do* something. Your father keeps you so busy, and I am wary of overstaying my welcome with Hannah's family. I suppose I just thought that everything would be settled once we got to Oregon, but that day still seems so far away."

"But we're getting there, my love. Every day there's progress, even if it's hard to see."

"I know." She sighed. "I'm sure you're right. I'm just . . . I feel useless and frustrated and like I'm being left behind."

"I don't mean to leave you behind. I'm so sorry you

feel that way. Maybe I'll send Abby over to keep you company."

"I'm sure your sister is lovely, but from what you've told me she's even more independent than I am. I haven't even gotten a chance to spend time with her, she's been off on her own so much. I can't imagine her needing anything from me that can keep me busy enough. Please understand . . . I'm not blaming you. But it feels like I am so close to not living in the Sullivans' wagon anymore, and yet I have no idea when I'll be out of here."

"Well, you don't want to live with my parents, do you?"

"Um . . . I—I don't want to seem ungrateful, but . . ." She blushed, laughing awkwardly.

"Exactly," Daniel said with a grin. "Me either. But that just means we have to wait a few more months— probably not even that long—until I can build us a house. It could just be a handful of weeks, if everything goes well. And then, I promise, the very first thing I am going to do is marry you. I'll do it in my shirtsleeves and holding a hammer if that's what it takes. But I want to have a home to give you. A home of your own."

"A home of my own," Caroline repeated.

"Of *our* own."

"You do know I've never had to keep house before in my life, don't you?" she asked worriedly. "I've learned to cook a bit while on the trail, and laundry, but not much else. How often do you suppose a person should sweep her floor?"

Daniel chuckled. "We can figure that out together, I think. If nothing else, I'm sure we could get Hannah to make you a list. Keeping the floor spotless is the last thing I'm going to worry about."

"We need a floor first, I suppose."

"We do. I'll tell you what. Tomorrow, before supper, you and I will go choose our homestead. Is that all right? Or would you prefer I find us a place on my own?"

"No, please let me come. I know it is just one small first step, but at least I'll feel as though we've really started then. I'll feel like I'm doing something instead of just waiting."

"Nothing is more important to me than putting your mind at ease. Tomorrow, then. And in the meantime, I'm going to go vote that our town be named Eden-something."

Caroline laughed. "If you all end up with 'Eden *Something*,' please don't tell anyone it was my idea."

CHAPTER FOUR

Though she was so excited that she had a difficult time falling asleep, the following morning Caroline was up before the sun. She wanted to ensure she had enough time to gather and heat the water she needed to wash thoroughly before Daniel came to collect her for their outing. She could not be more eager about the prospect of seeking out her future home and wanted everything to be perfect. It wasn't as ideal as she might have hoped for, but she could be grateful to have a clean dress, since Hannah had done the family's laundry only a couple days earlier.

"You look radiant," Hannah said when she climbed out of the Sullivans' sleeping wagon not long after sunrise. "When he sees you, Daniel will insist on marrying you on the spot."

"I hope not," she responded with a laugh as she dried her face. "At the very least I want to wash my hair first."

As Hannah set about making breakfast, Caroline tried to stay calm. She was grateful to her friend for taking over the cooking; she was afraid that in her distraction she might burn herself or the food.

This, she reminded herself, was the first day of the rest of her life. Everything was happening.

Daniel and Caroline had not set a specific time for him to come fetch her, and as the morning wore on she grew more and more anxious, worried that he had been delayed or that his father had required something more of him.

"It's not even nine in the morning, Caroline," Hannah said soothingly when she had paced by for the ninth time. "There's no need to get yourself worked up."

But she couldn't sit still. The next twenty minutes felt like hours as she paced back and forth, watching the direction in which she thought he would arrive. When she finally spotted Daniel's profile against the morning sun, she breathed a sigh of relief.

He approached the Sullivans' wagons riding his own horse and leading another.

"What's this?"

"I didn't think about this last night when we discussed it," he told her, "but I hope you can ride all right. I had totally forgotten that we obviously wouldn't be taking a wagon, and it's not as though there are a number of buggies we can borrow. Walking all the way out there would take too long. This horse is borrowed from the Kirks; her name is Peanut. We'll have to get you your own soon, I guess."

"Oh, I . . ." Caroline was flustered. "I haven't ridden in so long, and it wasn't very common in New York. But I think I can manage. Just . . . don't leave me."

"I never would."

He dismounted so he could help her up.

"Your hands will be just ruined from those reins," Hannah pointed out pessimistically. "It's a shame all our gloves have been worn through long ago."

"There's not much softness left of my hands to protect," Caroline responded. She wrapped her shawl around her shoulders, tying the corners in a tight knot in front to ensure it stayed on, and stepped up into the saddle.

"Hope you don't mind riding astride," Daniel said.

"No, of course not." Caroline swallowed hard. "I've never done it though. Can we go slow?"

He beamed at her, proud of her courage and her willingness to try. At the sight of such obvious approval, Caroline stifled a giggle. She was thinking about Philip Ross, a scion of New York society, and what he—and his mother—would have thought about Miss Caroline Harper riding astride a horse. She had been so sure that she would marry that man and go on to rule New York society, and now here she was with callused palms, a leg on either side of a horse—even-tempered though it may be—and off to explore through acres that had not been seen by any white woman yet.

"Ready?" Daniel asked, having mounted his own horse.

When she nodded, he nudged his horse off toward the trail that was quickly becoming established between all the wagons and scattered campsites. Caroline carefully nudged her own mare after him, but the animal seemed well used to it; Peanut seemed, in fact, to *want* to follow Daniel's horse. Caroline needn't have worried.

Once they got outside the circle of camps, Daniel slowed his horse so that he rode alongside her.

"Would you like to see a few different options for our future home, or should we just go to the one I'm most excited about?"

There was a twinkle in his eye. Caroline loved to see him so enthusiastic.

"The one you like best, I think. I don't want to take up more of your day than I need to."

"You're never taking up my day, Caroline. But Pa was hoping I would be back in time to help him start building a smaller, more everyday wagon. Let's go to just the one homestead for now. It's about ten minutes or so from here."

They rode in silence, though Caroline wanted to ask all manner of questions. There were no roads here, however, and only the smallest hint of a trail here and there where Indian tribes had come before. Daniel led the way, slowly picking through the tall grass, around the stones hidden therein and over tiny rivulets of streams that crisscrossed the land. Even this late in the autumn season, so much around them was green.

It really did seem as though Oregon was the haven that Caroline's brother had hoped for when he packed them both up to head west.

As she followed carefully behind Daniel, Caroline allowed her thoughts to roam to memories of her brother. After he had lost all of their family's business back in New York City, he had insisted their only option was to start over again on the west coast. If he had lived long enough to get here, Caroline might not even be settling in this new town with Daniel. Her brother, John, had wanted to start a new shipping business; he would have dragged her farther west, to Portland, or north to Puget Sound.

"Wait," Daniel said, pulling her out of her memories.

He had stopped in the middle of a thin grove of pine trees. When Caroline looked up and saw where they were, she felt a deep peace fall over her. It was cool and dark in these trees, and though she couldn't see far past them, she felt safe.

"Here?"

"No, I want to make sure you have the best first impression. We'll tie the horses and walk from here."

After he had helped her down off the horse, Daniel made her promise to keep her eyes closed. She was amused by his insistence on ceremony, but happy to go along.

"Just don't leave me," she said, peeking at him one last time before closing her eyes tight.

He took both her hands in his and pulled her gently toward him. "Just follow the sound of my voice," he said.

She only stumbled on sticks and stones a couple times before she could feel the tall grass under her feet and guessed that the grove was behind them. After a few more steps, Caroline felt the sun on her face.

Daniel stopped. "All right, open your eyes."

She did, blinking against the sun and letting her eyes adjust to the light. She took a deep breath, taking in the fresh scents of fall in the Pacific Northwest. Looking around, she was thrilled to see what seemed like the perfect place for a home. There was a wide-open area, bright with sun that would grow the vegetables they could eat every day. That backed up to another stand of trees that would give them the fuel and protection to live here a long time. One of the older trees appeared to have died and was leaning down almost horizontally, and Caroline had a vision of small boys—boys with Daniel's hair color—climbing and playing along the tree's length.

"What do you think?" Daniel asked softly.

Caroline held her breath.

"I thought, maybe, the house in this flat spot here," he said, gesturing. He walked forward a few steps. "We'll dig a well, of course, but there's also a small stream about three quarters of a mile that way"—he pointed—"through the trees. I think it will probably be the boundary between farms."

She looked up at him and beamed. "I've only ever lived on cobblestone streets, you know. What do you do with a stream just at the edge of your property?"

"I know. I'm sure we can figure it out together."

"What else?" she said eagerly, looking around the space and trying to picture the structures and animals that would fill it soon.

"A barn, maybe back here a ways." He gestured toward the edge of the trees. "North is that way, so this side of the house is probably best for your kitchen garden. And then fields beyond that in the other direction. We can claim a few hundred acres. Plenty to support a family. We'll have to take out a bunch of the trees, and I imagine there will be a number of stones that come up when we start tilling, but it's a start. Little by little."

"I can just picture it."

Caroline looked out over the landscape. This would be her home. This would be the horizon where she watched the sun set every evening. This would be where she waited for her husband to return at the end of the day.

This would be her home.

She just needed to be patient.

"How soon do you think we can get something built?"

Daniel shook his head. "Not right away. But just securing the location will be a good first step. And then maybe Ben and I can come clear space little by little while the rest of the town gets built up."

"Oh."

"And my parents are talking about taking the lot just west of this one. There's more clear land that way, so Pa will have less hard labor to do right at first. I think Mama is looking forward to being close to us. She still doesn't seem to quite believe I'm getting married. She keeps asking if I'm sure." He chuckled.

Caroline froze. "Oh," she said again. She cleared her throat. "Really? I thought . . . I thought she likes me."

"She does, as much as she knows you. I think she knows more about John, to be honest, what with as much trouble as he caused my father."

Caroline's face burned with shame. Her brother had set out on the Oregon Trail so full of enthusiasm, but the reality had worn him down. His problems with drinking and gambling had all but broken her heart, making every day of survival even harder than it needed to be. Which meant of course that the wagon company captain, Daniel's father, had had to manage the fallout of John's mistakes and selfishness.

"Well, I guess I'll need to spend more time with your

mother," Caroline said, trying to sound light. "Have her over for tea and cake, or something."

Daniel chuckled. "I'm sure she loves you, tea or no. Mama isn't always easy to read. Abby claims she doesn't like *her* either."

"Her own daughter?"

He shrugged. "I try to stay out of it. But you and Mama will be fine. Especially living here as neighbors. And you'll have plenty of time to get to know each other. Once we're married."

"Once we're married," Caroline repeated, feeling her anxiety melt away.

He looked deep into her eyes, smiled, and wrapped his arm around her shoulders, pulling her to him.

"But you like it? Should I tell my father this is the homestead for us?"

Caroline took one last look around, taking it all in, then leaned her head on his shoulder and wrapped her own arm around his waist. John Harper was gone, and the shame and trouble that he had caused her was also leaving. Her duty now was to honor his memory, and the best way to do that would be to plunge head first into this new life in the Oregon Territory.

"Yes, please," she told Daniel. "This is our home."

CHAPTER FIVE

"I want to get a spot near the front," Hannah said excitedly.

She linked her arm through Caroline's as they walked in a group toward the water's edge. Martha Sullivan held Caroline's hand, while Patience held Hannah's, and Junior escorted his mother. Together they joined the crowd of settlers making their way to the center of what would be their new town on the river.

As she looked around at her friends and neighbors, Caroline had to remind herself that only a just one short week earlier they were all camped high in the mountains, nearly starving and hopeless that they would ever make it to the Oregon Territory. Though many were still thin and weak, the smiling, hopeful faces all around her buoyed Caroline.

It seemed as though the worst was truly behind them.

The Sullivans had left their camp too late to get a spot at the front of the crowd, but Hannah put the little girls in front of her and they all nudged their way through the group so they could hear what was being said. The vote on what to name their town had taken place two evenings prior, and Mr. Mills had organized this meeting to mark the exciting occasion of the town's founding.

The first steps on clearing this main part of town where the bridge would go had already started. The tall, monumental ponderosa remained, but three of the nearby trees had been felled in the previous day; Mr. Mills stood tall on one of the wide tree stumps that had not yet been pulled up. He waved his hat over his head in broad strokes, drawing people to him, and reminding Caroline somehow of the American flag, flying high above the forts they had passed on their way to Oregon.

"Good evening," he called out over the settlers. "Come closer! Gather in, now."

Caroline felt Miss Atkins, the schoolteacher, take a step closer to her behind her left shoulder. Little Apollo Robinson was at her elbow, the rest of his family just behind.

"Can you see okay?" she asked, leaning down to the little boy.

Apollo nodded, smiling with excitement, and Caroline turned her attention back to Mr. Mills.

"Now, I'm not much one for speeches"—many men in the crowd laughed at this self-deprecatory falsehood —"but I must say it is truly remarkable to see all of you gathered here, looking up at me as we take the very first steps to conquer this new land."

A few errant cheers floated from the crowd around her.

"I'm sure you agree with me that the path here has been arduous. We have lost loved ones. We have sacrificed more than any man, woman, or child should ever have to. But we have made it. And our reward, as you see, is this veritable paradise, in a territory that we can make our own, building a home and eventually, yes, a state and a nation for our children and our children's children."

He paused, as though overcome with emotion, and a spattering of applause filled the silence.

"And now, without any more hedging or teasing . . ."

He paused again, waiting a long, pregnant moment while the crowd looked on expectantly.

"Welcome to Eden Valley, Oregon," he declared with another flourish of his wide hat. The gasps and cries of delight in the crowd around Caroline warmed her heart. "I would like to thank my son's future wife, Miss Caroline Harper, for setting us down the path with the suggestion of the word *eden*. Once Daniel mentioned it at our meeting the other night, nearly all the debate ceased, and we knew we had found our home."

He scanned the crowed, looking for Caroline, who stood with the Sullivans about a third of the way through the crowd, and once he had found her he beamed.

"Eden Valley will be as a beacon on a hill. I hope we can all come together, as we have every day since leaving Independence, and make this a community of like-minded individuals, all striving toward united goals."

A bright round of applause broke out throughout the crowd. Caroline raised her chin with a wide smile, proud to have been of any help at all. Creativity had never been a strength of hers, and yet here she was leaving a legacy, just in helping name her new home.

Hannah grinned at her as they clapped wildly.

"And now, with that out of the way," Mr. Mills continued, "it's officially down to business. Mr. Findley has some announcements."

He stepped down, gesturing to the other man who had been waiting at his side.

Mr. Findley stood up on the tree stump, almost losing his balance in the process. He cleared his throat, glanced down at his notes, and looked back out over the families gathered.

"I'm sure you're all eager to get a roof over your heads," he began. "We think that if we can all simply organize and direct our resources, we should be settled as soon as possible. There are some priorities that need to be made first, as I think you'll agree, but little by little we will get it all done.

"The first thing we want to take care of is building a church for Pastor Montgomery, as well as a parsonage for his family. We'll also prioritize a forge for Mr. Gilroy, and a general store for Mr. Jameson. That's where we plan to also house the post office when we can get the United States to recognize us, with a wire service in the meantime. Eventually we will also begin work on a school before next fall, as well as a town hall and any other public buildings we decide are needed, but these will be the start.

"I know this all sounds grand." He raised his hands to quiet the excited murmuring that rippled through the crowd. "We've got a long way to go, of course, but the better we start, the better we can continue, both safely and efficiently.

"Beyond those public buildings, each man—each family—has been tasked with informing me of the size of home they are planning to build, which we will then coordinate with the surveyor and help each family make their official claims with the government. And from there we can share labor around. I know, for example, Mrs. Buchanan would be mighty grateful for any help, seeing as her oldest boy is a mere five years old."

Many in the crowd laughed at that. Caroline, remembering that Daniel would be taking care of all of it for both of them, felt a wave of gratitude. He would make sure they had their home; he would make sure she didn't have to worry about anything. She wanted to help, of course, but she needn't stress herself with it.

"Many of you have begun scouting out the surrounding farmland and staking your claims. Just a reminder to come see Mr. Mills or myself when you have made decisions. This might be the lawless west"—he grinned—"but we're aiming to make all of this as easy as possible. The more we can work together, the better for everyone.

"And I think that's all for the official announcements. Mr. Mills?"

Mr. Findley climbed down, awkwardly again, as he yielded the floor to Daniel's father.

"Thank you, Findley." He returned to his position, again looking out over the crowd of emigrants gathered.

"There's just one more thing I wanted to mention. In addition to the other public establishments, Mrs. Mills is founding a women's temperance society, with the aim to help keep our young men from wasting their time and money on such a vice as alcohol. Though such an organization might seem frivolous when we're all still trying to build houses before the winter, we are of the mind that this will help us start out our community of Eden Valley strong."

Most of the crowd had already started to break up as Mr. Mills finally finished, though Caroline listened to the very end, wondering if her own brother's behavior was a motivation behind Mrs. Mills starting a temperance society. The knowledge that her future mother-in-law was wary of her brought back all the memories of what Caroline had been through in New York, how Philip's mother had tried to warn her off her son. Was there something wrong with her that made mothers so protective?

Caroline glanced at Mrs. Sullivan, who had so graciously taken her into her home and family with no complaint.

No, this must just be an unfortunate coincidence. Caroline was determined to not let Mrs. Mills—or, most importantly, Daniel—down. She would be everything a prospective daughter should be. She would prove that she was worthy.

All around her the other settlers moved away, some heading back to their own camp, others meeting up with friends to talk over the news of the evening. Nearest the water, she spotted Jasper Stephens, the blacksmith's apprentice, flirting with Nora Cole. Seen walking away in the other direction was Annie Hudson, with one arm linked through that of her nephew Lawrence; that boy had gotten so much taller since they had left Independence. Junior was gathered with a group of four other young men, all glancing slyly at a cluster of some of the young ladies, including Abby Mills and Katie Valentine. Even from this distance, Caroline could see that the girls were trying to pretend they didn't know they were being watched, even as they tossed their heads enticingly.

"Shall we head back?" Hannah said, returning Caroline's attention to her. "Ben told me he and Daniel would be busy going around to all the camps, answering questions and collecting mail to be taken to the fort. We probably won't see them more tonight."

"Oh." Caroline looked around for Daniel, hoping he could tell her about his evening himself, but she couldn't see his tall, broad shoulders anywhere. "Yes, I suppose we'd better."

But just as she was about to turn away, Caroline's eye caught Daniel's, over the heads of most of the crowd gathered, tall as he was. He was with Mr. Gilroy, the two of them about to walk in the opposite direction of her. He smiled, waved cheerfully, and turned back to the man he had been talking to.

As she too turned to walk away, Caroline tried not to let Hannah hear her disappointed sigh.

While the public buildings of Eden Valley were being built, and while the citizens spread out across the countryside to choose their future land and make homes, most of the families that had come west on the trail had formed a makeshift camp about half a mile from the tree stump where Mr. Mills had made his announcement. Caroline and Hannah trailed behind Mrs. Sullivan, who held the hands of the little Sullivan girls, Patience and Martha.

"Is Junior not coming?" Caroline asked when she realized he wasn't with them.

"Oh." Hannah looked back over her shoulder. "Maybe he needed to talk to Mr. Mills or someone. Congratulations on naming the town, though," she said, turning her attention back to Caroline. "That's quite an accomplishment. I'm so proud!"

"If I ever start bemoaning being useless, remind me that I did do that one thing," she responded with a grin.

CHAPTER SIX

Little by little, the Sullivan–Mills wagon company settled in to their little corner of the valley. From dawn till dusk, every moment was full of work, each person frantically trying to get as settled as they could before winter weather set in. The sooner this all was completed, the sooner they could, once and for all, be done living out of covered wagons. Clearing land, digging wells, stripping logs, foraging for wild vegetables, laying foundations for the structures that would be going up—the process seemed unending.

For Caroline, every day was exhausting, but in a very different way than it had been while walking west on the Oregon Trail. Where before trudging westward each day had seemed endless with little hint of the progress they were making, now Caroline saw evidence of everyone's hard work everywhere she looked. Trees came down; walls went up. In the morning there would be a broad meadow, and by the time the sun set, that same stretch of ground would be cleared to the dirt with at least half a dozen trees stacked and ready to be used as lumber.

Caroline wanted nothing more than to be helpful. She had been so proud of everything she had learned and everything she had done during the months on the Oregon Trail, but now that families were getting more settled, she felt lost. Daniel was too busy to help direct her as to how she could make progress on their own homestead, and Mrs. Sullivan—as the widow of one of their captains—had more assistance from the community than she needed. Hannah was often busy with Benjamin Findley and their own homestead.

Caroline felt useless.

After several days passed like this, Caroline realized that despite all her growth since leaving New York, she still could barely take care of herself without at least a little guidance, and she hadn't made more than a couple real friends among the company.

It was enough to make her lose hope all over again.

She kept such disappointments to herself, however. It wouldn't do to dampen the enthusiasm of the ones she loved just because she felt a bit helpless.

As such, Caroline was baking an extra couple batches of biscuits late one morning at the Sullivan family camp when Daniel came by looking for her.

"You look bored," he said with a wink. "Need a project?"

"Yes!" she said adamantly. "Biscuits I know how to do, at least, but if you have something—anything—else you think I would be fit for, I am all ears."

"I was kidding about the project"—Caroline tried not to let her disappointment show at these words—

"but I'm sure your biscuits are exactly what Mrs. Sullivan needs. Come to supper tonight," he said. "Granted, it will still be over a campfire, but my mother has acquired a few more supplies than just beans and bacon."

"And biscuits?"

"Yes," he said with a laugh.

"You're sure I won't be an inconvenience?"

"Absolutely not. Remember, I told you my mother needed to get to know you. This will be the perfect first step."

Caroline nodded, resolved. "Yes, then. Thank you. I'd love to. And in the meantime, find me a project, would you? I hate feeling useless."

Throughout the rest of that day, Caroline was restless and distracted. At one point, while trying to focus on repairing a hole in her apron, she managed to ask Hannah three separate times when the Jamesons were going to have another dance before she actually registered her friend's answer.

"What has gotten into you?" Hannah asked. "This invite tonight is just supper over a campfire like you've been doing for months already."

"I'm not sure I've spoken more than a few sentences to Mrs. Mills," Caroline said. "And I've had trouble with my suitor's mother in the past. I'm petrified she won't like me."

"Daniel is not just some suitor," Hannah assured her. "And this is a very different situation than when you were in New York. I don't know what happened back then, but everything will be fine tonight. Daniel wouldn't invite you if he was worried about it."

Caroline nodded and tried to turn her attention back to her sewing.

Later, when Daniel arrived again to walk her back to his family's camp, she was careful to keep her tone light, betraying none of the agony she had put herself through that day. They talked about the blacksmith's forge that was being built, and how long he thought it might take for the town to have real mail delivery. Daniel was so involved with the building and establishment of Eden Valley that Caroline almost felt accomplished by proxy. That was her beau who was doing so much for this community.

As they finally approached the Mills family's camp, she felt shy. Abby, Daniel's younger sister, and Mrs. Mills were both crowding around the campfire, tending to the pair of pots that bubbled and cooked there. She didn't see Mr. Mills immediately, but then he emerged from one of the family's wagons with a rocking chair hoisted over his head.

Daniel hurried forward to help his father while Caroline held back.

Mr. Mills took the chair back from Daniel once he had both feet on the ground and brought it over to the campfire, closer to where the rest of the family was sitting.

"Come sit, Miss Harper," the big man said, extending his hand to her. "It's not much, but as our welcome guest, it's yours."

"Oh, no, I couldn't. It's your only chair."

"Don't be silly. Sit," Mrs. Mills said. A little gruffly, Caroline thought, but she obeyed.

The rocking chair creaked as she sank back in its

deep wooden seat. This would be awkward and uncomfortable, trying to eat with a plate balanced on her knees while sitting in a chair that literally moved underneath her, but Caroline reminded herself that the Millses were being hospitable. They were trying to offer her comfort.

She would just have to smile and do her best.

"Thank you."

"And how did you spend your day, dear?" Mrs. Mills asked as she handed Caroline a plate and silverware.

She looked down at the generous spread of pan-fried steak and mashed potatoes. They must have butchered another of their herd. The Millses had driven a few dozen cattle west to Oregon, and though not all the animals had made it the full two thousand miles, enough had so as to afford the family a measure of wealth that many of the other settlers could only dream of. It was subtle, but apparent, in the fare that Mrs. Mills had offered their guest.

Abby sat down on Caroline's left, looking up at her with mischievous eyes. "Yes, Miss Harper," she said in a tone full of sarcasm, "what fascinating excursion did you partake in this fine day?"

Caroline grinned at her; somehow it didn't feel as though she were being pitied or teased. She had an idea that Abby may have put in a similarly tedious day.

"Biscuits," she answered. "And sewing. A grand old time."

"You don't enjoy homemaking?" Mrs. Mills asked as she handed her husband his own full plate of food.

"Oh, I do. But, I guess I'm just feeling a little lost." Caroline shrugged self-consciously. "There's always something to do, of course, but I feel like there are ways

I could be more useful. I don't want to just wait around until it's time for me to get married, but I don't feel as though there are many ways that I can easily contribute. It's not as though I'm any good with a hammer or saw."

"Oh, I'm sure that's not true," Mr. Mills said, patting her hand kindly. "I imagine Mrs. Sullivan is mighty grateful for your help."

"She is. But she also has Hannah. Though, I suppose if Hannah gets married before me, I'll be of more use."

Caroline tried to keep any hint of impatience out of her tone, and she averted her eyes from Daniel's. Making him feel like he was being blamed for anything was the last thing she wanted to do, especially in front of his mother.

"You'll find your place," he said. "It's only been a few days, and there will be new things that need to be done every day."

Caroline nodded, and there was a brief silence as she took a bite of her potatoes.

"Ma wants me to go back to school," Abby interjected. "I told her I'd rather become a seamstress like Louisa Hudson, or get married like you, but she didn't seem to like that option either. Probably because I don't even have a beau."

"You could always join the temperance society," Mr. Mills said to Caroline, seeming to ignore his daughter's teasing outburst. "Or start some other community organization of your own. Though I wonder at my wife being able to manage her own commitment to so much outside the house. I would hate to wish that on someone else."

"Yes, why don't you join the temperance society, Miss

Harper? Surely your insight must be valuable given all you've gone through with your brother." Mrs. Mills gazed at her with an expression Caroline couldn't read.

"Oh . . . well, maybe," Caroline responded, though she was struck with a memory of feeling stuck in New York parlors that made her shrink away from the suggestion. "I had something more . . . tangible in mind. I'm afraid I don't much know what a temperance society might do."

"We will spend most of our time educating the community about the evils of alcohol and spirits. Eventually we'll hold fundraisers or other events to raise awareness of the dreaded affliction. Of course, I am not impractical. I know that such a society while we are all still living in tents might be considered frivolous." She smiled. "But I mean that we should begin as we mean to go on, and found Eden Valley on the sober, steadfast principles that will guide our town to become a beacon in the Oregon Territory."

"Maybe you should be the one making speeches instead of me, my love," Mr. Mills said with a grin.

"Don't you even think about it, George. When you are elected mayor, I will be standing in the background, smiling, so that all attention is directed at you."

"Mayor?" Caroline prompted, looking between them.

"You didn't tell her?" Abby asked her brother.

"We want Eden Valley to be reputable and established as soon as possible," Daniel explained. "So my father and Mr. Findley are going to call for an election in the next month or so. First for mayor, then sheriff."

"And eventually a city council," Mr. Mills added. "Maybe even our own judge one day."

"Now don't go getting ahead of yourself," his wife said with an indulgent smile. "They don't even have a judge in Portland yet."

"But that town is due to be incorporated officially in a few months, and after that, who knows what could happen? This could be part of a new state one day."

"My father has a lot of big dreams," Daniel told Caroline in a carrying whisper.

"I think it's lovely," she averred. "Didn't we all come west because of big dreams?"

"Exactly right, my dear," Mr. Mills said, beaming at her.

She caught Daniel looking at her in a similarly admiring way, and she held his gaze.

"Caroline, do *you* have any big dreams?" Abby asked boldly. "Didn't your brother run a shipping company back east?"

"Yes, he took over when I was small, after our parents died. I think he had intended to start a similar company here, but then . . ." She cleared her throat and shook off the sorrow that threatened to overwhelm her.

"Oh?" said Abby, interested. "A family business? Would you be interested in doing something similar? Like Louisa Hudson did, build your independence completely?"

Caroline laughed awkwardly and looked at Daniel, who fortunately did not seem the least bit offended that his sister was encouraging her to not need him. "No," she said. "I can honestly say it never occurred to me. I didn't really have anything to do with the business in New York. I wouldn't even know where to start."

"Oh," Abby said again, disappointed now.

"Abby, stop questioning our guest's every decision," her father said. "The idea that she would have come out here to start a shipping company by herself is . . . well, it's certainly not an easy assumption to make."

Daniel changed the subject then, telling Caroline more about what their own life had been like back east, with the hundreds of head of cattle they were responsible for on top of all the rest of the moving parts of a family farm. The idea of getting so much from the land just outside her door was completely foreign to Caroline, and she spent the rest of the evening peppering the Mills family with questions in between bites.

Finally, about an hour after dark, Abby spoke up.

"Daniel, are you walking Caroline back to her camp or is, um, anyone coming to meet her?"

"Are you that eager to get rid of her, Abby?" he asked. "Or is that a hint for the dessert Mama baked?"

"No." She shrugged. "I was just wondering."

"We have freshly baked cookies," he said, confiding in Caroline. "Why don't I walk you back after that?"

"Perfect."

She settled back into the rocking chair and tried to ignore the growing expression of disappointment crossing his mother's face.

CHAPTER SEVEN

The following night, Hannah brought the family's narrow looking glass out from under the wagon canopy and hung it from a bent nail on the outside of the canvas along one of the ribs.

"I never trust how I look under there," she told Caroline as she took down her hair to run her fingers through. "There's not nearly enough light. At least here we still have a few minutes of light before sunset."

"Is Junior coming to the dance?"

"Last I heard, he was. I think he might have his eyes on one of the young ladies, but he won't tell me who. All I know is I found him heating water for a bath this morning, and I'm not sure that has ever happened before without Ma nagging him for a full day."

Caroline laughed. She watched her friend tilt her head this way and that, checking her reflection in the small mirror. "He's getting to be a young man, you know, Hannah. He's not your baby brother anymore."

"Believe me, I know. He keeps reminding me. 'You

shouldn't talk to me like that, Hannah. I'm the *man* of the house now!' Or so he wants us all to think."

"He's really grown up so much in these weeks since your father died, hasn't he?"

"Yes." Hannah softened and turned to Caroline. "I know I make fun, but . . . I really am so proud of Junior. He'll be seventeen in a couple months, but it seems like he's had to take on more responsibilities than men ten years older. Plus, he'll walk us over to the dance and home again, since Ben is busy. *And* he'll smell clean. I can't be too irritated with him."

"Daniel will be meeting me there too," Caroline answered lightly. "I'm so grateful he has the time."

The day that Daniel had taken her to see the acres he wanted to claim for them had been the last time she had really felt as though he'd paid any attention to her. She was trying to not be too needy, but everything was moving so fast. It was easy to feel as though she were being left behind. Even when she'd had supper with the Mills family a couple nights earlier, she had felt as though she had been invited for the sole purpose of being judged by his mother, rather than to spend any real time with her betrothed.

Hannah stepped aside so Caroline could use the glass, and Caroline also took down her hair and brushed it out while checking her reflection in the mirror. She leaned closer to the glass to look for freckles or sunburn that might mar her fair skin. Though it had taken her some time while on the trail to agree to wearing a bonnet, now she wouldn't go without it. The wide brim protected her face quite well.

"You look lovely," Hannah said, watching her. "Daniel is already crazy about you."

"We should go soon," Junior said, approaching the girls. "It's kind of a long walk."

"We're going to build or buy another wagon before we move out to the farm, right? A smaller one we can ride in around town?" Hannah asked.

"You'll be married before then. Ask your man. But, yes. I wouldn't make Ma and the girls walk miles into town. What kind of man do you take me for?" He winked as he sauntered off.

"Are you and Ben any closer to setting a date?" Caroline asked as she finished pinning up her hair again.

Hannah sighed. "Yes and no. I think we might actually be closer than he's willing to tell me, because he doesn't want me to get my hopes up just in case it all fails. But . . ." She smiled. "Soon. I think. I *hope*. Maybe a few weeks."

"Come on, ladies!" Junior called impatiently.

"All right, all right," Hannah called back, smoothing down her skirt one last time.

The sun had completely set by now, but the light of campfires lit their path as the trio made their way between campsites.

Whether intentionally or by design, when the company of settlers chose a general campsite for their wagons and animals in the interim before houses were built, the Jameson men were settled to the far edge of the cluster. All through the six months they had traveled west, Martin Jameson had regularly brought out his fiddle to offer the displaced Americans some relief, joy, and small reminder of home. Here in Oregon, it seemed as though he would continue on the same. So, as Caroline, Hannah, and Junior made their way across the scattered wagons to the far side where the Jamesons had their camp, the bright music, laughter, and chatter of other young people tempted them.

As they drew closer, Caroline felt Junior straighten up next to her, as though trying to look as tall as possible. She glanced at him and noticed his whole expression had brightened. Grinning, she nudged Hannah on her other side and directed her attention to her brother. The two girls kept their mouths shut, not wanting to let on that they so plainly saw a change in him. But Caroline was deeply curious about what such a display could mean.

Caroline didn't have a chance to scan the crowd in front of them to see who Junior was puffing up for before Ben Findley hurried forward to meet Hannah.

"Ben!" she exclaimed, all but falling into his arms.

Caroline watched them with a smile. This man made her best friend so happy; it was easy to see their intimacy, their companionship. She really could not be happier for Hannah.

"Quick," he said, pulling his fiancée's hand. "I've convinced the band to play a waltz, but we have to get over there in time."

Hannah waved at her friend and brother over her shoulder as Ben led her to the dance floor.

Junior leaned close to Caroline. "I'll walk you home in a couple hours?" he asked, though his attention was clearly elsewhere.

"Go," Caroline told him. "Have fun. I'm sure Daniel

will find me soon, and then Hannah and I will come find you when we're ready to leave."

With no response but a grin, Junior ducked away into the crowd of young people. Caroline watched him for a moment, curious. As long as she had known Junior Sullivan, he had been a mini version of his father, focused on his responsibilities and taking care of his family as best he could. Paradoxically, now that his father was gone and he had even more responsibilities, Junior seemed to be letting loose a little bit more. Joking more, having fun. She wasn't sure he had gone to any of the dances that the wagon company had when they were on the Oregon Trail.

But no sooner did Junior dash to his friends than Daniel appeared at Caroline's side.

"There you are!" she said. "I've been all alone for the longest time."

"I just saw Junior leave," he said pointedly. "You don't fool me, Miss Harper."

"All right, then. It just *felt* like the longest time because I've missed you."

"Never fear. I'm here now, ready to squire you about all evening. Have you had supper? Should we get a drink? Or dancing?"

"Dancing," she replied promptly with a wide smile. "I missed too many chances over the last year, and I regret it so."

Daniel didn't comment as he led her to the dance floor, though they both knew why she had missed chances to dance. Hannah had tried to convince her, to break her out of her shell. To Caroline, in those first months of mourning the loss of her life in New York and the loss of her wealth, and then later when she was mourning her brother, the idea of dancing in a dirt clearing to a fiddle with a man who just hours earlier had been handling oxen was simply beyond what she could handle. It was too far of a jump for her.

She had learned a lot since leaving Missouri, both about herself and about other people who on the surface seemed so different from her. And now the idea of spending a Saturday evening dancing with her betrothed —a man for whom she could not wait to cook in a home of their own—was the only thing worth doing that night. She beamed at Daniel as he put one hand on her waist and led her in the first steps.

The music sounded different this night than it had over the summer along the Oregon Trail. Caroline looked more carefully at the musicians and realized that one of the men from Dempsey—one of the unmarried bachelors who had rescued the company and then stuck around to help—was sitting in with the rest of the musicians. He held a large jug to his lips, blowing into it rhythmically, giving the whole song a grounding bass sound. Martin Jameson played the fiddle, Davis Waters strummed a guitar, Joe Larson huffed into a harmonica, and Billy Whitson held his mother's washboard.

Daniel whirled her around and around. He was a far better dancer than Caroline would have guessed, and being led through all the steps in his strong arms was almost like floating.

Her attention was caught by a canoodling couple in the dim light near the Jamesons' wagon, over Daniel's shoulder. The gangly figure looked familiar, as did the shorter one, and she realized that was Junior Sullivan leaning his tall body over Abby Mills. She seemed to look around as though wary of being seen, before turning all her attention to beam enamoredly up into Junior's face.

Caroline opened her mouth to point out the couple, but closed it again. Something about the way Abby was holding herself, as though trying to appear at a distance from Junior while still leaning close, told Caroline that she was perhaps not supposed to see what she had just seen. As the song ended, she looked up at Daniel and wondered if he had any idea that his younger sister was getting attention from young men, let alone that one in particular.

"I had to promise my mother I would give all day Monday to a trip out to Fort Vancouver before she relented on letting me come tonight," Daniel said, drawing Caroline's attention back.

"Daniel!" Caroline laughed. "You're how old? Twenty-five and about to get married. Did you really need your mother's permission?"

"No, not really, I suppose. It's just that everything is always easier when Mama is happy. Best to give her what she wants whenever I can."

"But that means you're going to be gone all day Monday. Or will it be longer than that? The fort is far, isn't it?"

He shrugged. "It needs to be done. And it will likely need to be done more in the future, so . . ." He sighed. "I'll be back Monday night. There's no need to worry."

"I just want you to stay safe."

"On the frontier of Oregon?" He laughed. "We might need to lower your expectations a bit."

She nudged him gently. "Don't joke, please. You know what I mean."

As the song ended, Daniel caught up both of her small hands in his and brought them to his mouth, kissing the palm of first one and then the other. "I promise to be as safe as I can."

"Thank you. I suppose that's as good as I'll get."

CHAPTER EIGHT

The first couple Sundays the pioneers spent in the Oregon Territory truly were days of rest. Coming down off the mountain on a Saturday, each person needed a full day with which to sleep and pray and give thanks for their deliverance. There was so much going on in the early days that the pastor made no attempt to lead any kind of official worship service. It was all anyone could do to sleep when they finally had the chance.

The morning after the Jamesons held a dance on the edge of camp was the third Sunday after they had settled in Oregon, Pastor Montgomery was done with waiting. He was eager to establish the routine and expectation for church. He was proud of his position as one of the pillars of the community and took such leadership seriously. Instead of a normal sermon, though, he used the Sunday morning gathering as a chance to break ground for the future church building.

Caroline and the Sullivans attended the groundbreaking along with most of the rest of Eden Valley.

With a short, prepared speech, Pastor Montgomery thanked the gathered congregants for all their support as they had traveled the Oregon Trail. He promised his church would be a sanctuary for all, and prayed that the building they were starting would be a monument to the faith and holiness of the community.

"Though the open expanse of God's creation will always be around us, in our memories and in our hearts," he concluded, "with us wherever we go, we still need a roof over our head, given how much it rains here."

There was an appreciative chuckle through the crowd.

Almost on cue, Caroline felt a light drop of water on the back of her hand. She looked up at the cloudy sky and was hit by two more drops.

"Now, don't be calling me a prophet," Pastor Montgomery joked over the murmuring of the crowd as everyone marveled at the timing of such a rain shower. "But if we hurry, we can break ground here before it all turns to mud. I've asked Mr. George Mills and his son, Daniel, to join me in turning over the first spade, as they have both been so integral to getting us to this place."

The two men hurried forward, ducking their heads against the light rain, and each accepted a shovel from Pastor Montgomery. Caroline watched with a burning pride; that was her beau, her future husband, who was so respected in the community to be asked to carry out such an important act.

The rain dripped off the men's hat brims. Pastor Montgomery grabbed a third shovel, and the three men each jabbed his tool into the dirt, right where the front steps of the future church would one day be.

Just as they turned over the dirt into a small pile to the side, the sky cleared and the sun shone down on the gathered congregation.

"Praise the Lord," the pastor said. He dropped his shovel and raised both hands in the air. "I don't think that sign could be any clearer. God looks down on our small community with favor and with grace! Thank you all for being here today. Let us pray."

His prayer was brief, but even so, with the final "Amen," Caroline was already feeling a few raindrops again. As the gathering broke up, she hurried back to the wagons with the rest of the Sullivans, and was pleased to find that Daniel had followed shortly behind them.

Though the rain wasn't heavy, Caroline and the Sullivans quickly holed up in their sleeping wagon to dry off. Daniel knocked lightly on the side of the wagon to announce his presence before sticking his head through the break in the canvas.

"Greetings, Sullivans," he said with a grin. "I won't stay long and track water into your wagon, but I just wanted to see if you all needed anything from the fort before I go tomorrow."

"Sugar," Patience said. "Please. Right, Ma?"

"I'm sure Daniel won't have room for all the sugar you want, dear," Mrs. Sullivan said before turning to him. "Really, any food would be helpful, but you don't have to do anything special for us."

"I'll do what I can. If I can manage it, my plan is to buy a wagon there and fill it with goods to bring back."

"That's smart," Caroline said.

"Then, when I return, I'm sure one of the men would

happily buy the wagon from me. Enough trips like that and we should have most of the town outfitted."

"How are you spending the rest of your Sunday?" Caroline asked, hoping to get some time with him before he was gone the entire day.

"Oh, Mama has a big meal planned. Something special, she says, before I'm gone the whole day, though I'm not sure how easy it will be for her if the rain doesn't let up. In fact, I should go. She has it in her head that I'll be risking my life traveling on my own tomorrow, and wants as much of me as she can get. I'll see you soon, all right, Caro?"

She nodded, trying to hide her disappointment that she hadn't been invited to the Mills family's special Sunday. Fortunately, Daniel ducked out again before noticing anything was amiss. As his fiancée, she, too, wanted as much of him as she could get. But, with each passing day, she felt less and less able to ask for it.

After he left, Hannah squeezed her hand sympathetically before asking her younger sisters, "All right, if we're going to have to be in the wagon most of the day . . . who wants to play a game?"

CHAPTER NINE

The following day, Monday, Caroline was determined to busy herself with something—anything—that could distract her and make her feel as though she was making progress. She didn't know what yet, but Daniel would be gone all day. It was a five- or six-hour ride to Fort Vancouver, after which he then needed to purchase supplies and make the same ride back, slower now with the weight of everything he was bringing home. She would count herself lucky if he wasn't too tired to see her on Tuesday.

She couldn't just sit and wait. But, much to her chagrin, Hannah was so full of energy herself that there was rarely anything around the Sullivan camp that needed doing.

Caroline loved to read and had brought several books west with her, but even those were becoming stale in the reading. She was tired of sitting still. She had to do *something*.

And so, instead, that Monday Caroline decided to

visit the claim that Daniel had showed her the previous week. She was fairly certain she could remember how to get there. Once there, she would figure out what came next.

Emerging from the family's wagon, Caroline tied on her bonnet and poured water into her canteen, preparing to set out for the day.

"Caroline? Where are you going?"

"I'm off to see my new home," she stated defiantly, as though daring Hannah to try to stop her.

"I thought Daniel was gone today."

"He is. I'm going to borrow the same horse from Mr. Kirk and go on my own. I know I can't very well cut down a tree or dig a well by myself, but I have to feel like I'm doing something, like some progress is being made. Surely there are stones and such that I can start to clear, right? Something? Even just . . . I don't know . . . walk around the acres and get to know my land."

Even Caroline could hear the desperation in her voice. This sitting-at-home-and-waiting was just not for her. Even when she had been in New York, completely incapable of keeping house, she had been involved in more than one charity organization, regularly invited to social events or galas, and kept plenty busy. Here in Oregon, she'd decided, she would be too.

"Do you want me to come with you?" Hannah asked. "I can tell Ben you need me today."

"No, no. No, thank you. I'm not sure it will amount to anything anyway. I don't want to take up your time."

Hannah peered at her with some concern but seemed to take her friend's words at face value. "All right, then. But if you're not back well before sunset, Junior is going to have your hide."

Caroline laughed, imagining an angry sixteen-year-old boy attempting to discipline her. "I promise."

"Be careful!" Hannah called after her.

She had not been with Daniel when he had borrowed the horse, Peanut, before. Now it took Caroline a good twenty minutes to convince Mr. Kirk that she would be perfectly fine on her own, both riding the horse astride and finding her way to and from the soon-to-be homestead. Finally, however, he just shook his head and gave in.

"You just make sure Daniel Mills knows it's your own fault if you get thrown and break a leg."

Caroline smiled stiffly. "Oh, I assure you, Mr. Kirk, Daniel is well aware of my stubbornness. Have you not heard about how I refused to wear a bonnet for the first several weeks on the trail?"

But even all that pleading was worth it in the end, when Caroline found herself riding the gentle mare out past the circle of wagons and into the Oregon countryside.

The narrow, barely visible trail she currently followed would one day be a wide road leading from the center of Eden Valley to her home. This same path would be her view as she returned home from church, or from a meeting at the town hall. Caroline took a deep breath and tried to sear this journey into her memory, as something to draw on in the years to come, something to point to as a reminder of how far she had come.

Since Daniel had insisted she keep her eyes closed while he brought her to the exact plot, Caroline almost rode right past the acres that were to be her home. It wasn't until she passed through the grove of trees where they had stopped previously that she realized the scene looked familiar: there was the dead tree, leaning almost down to the ground; there was the flat ground where Daniel predicted they should dig the well.

Directing the horse closer to the edge of the grove, Caroline reflected that riding astride was far easier than she had thought it would be. It was too bad the practice was considered so unladylike.

Not that anyone would see her all the way out here.

With that thought, for the first time Caroline realized how truly alone she was. She wondered if she was strictly safe. She had been so consumed with the idea of coming out here and getting something done that she had completely forgotten the fact that her future home was still technically the middle of the wilderness. She had no idea how nearby the closest Indian tribe might be. She had no idea if there were wild animals she might have to contend with, or even strange men passing by.

Caroline dismounted and stood next to the mare, looking over the green area where her house would be built, and lamented the fact that she had not brought a gun. She still had John's weapon packed away, though she hadn't touched it since he had died. She'd had a shooting lesson from Daniel all those months ago. Caroline Harper was capable of defending herself, more or less.

But not without a gun.

"Well, maybe we'll be back sooner than Hannah thinks, hmm?" she said to Peanut, stroking her snout.

But just as she had told Mr. Kirk, she was stubborn, and she wasn't about to head back having made no progress at all. So, instead, Caroline girded her loins and dug in.

As she strode across the tall grass, the ground felt firm beneath her feet. Other settlers' claims might be boggy or rocky, but the spot Daniel had picked out for them seemed just about perfect to her untrained eye. She moved to the center of the general area where Daniel had indicated their house could be built and looked around. Just as she had told Hannah, while there were limits to what she could do on her own, there was still something. Mentally mapping out a rough border of a building, Caroline soon identified an easy task for herself.

She spent the next couple hours moving rocks.

In no time, it seemed, she became aware of muscles in her back that she didn't know she had. And more than once did she wish for those same gloves Hannah had lamented the loss of just a few days earlier. But these things did not stop her. When she had been drinking tea served by silent butlers in luxurious New York sitting rooms, Caroline never would have dreamed how satisfying a day of manual labor could be. Though her hands got all scratched, front and back, she moved rock after rock to a pile well away from where the house would be built. Maybe they could be repurposed into a foundation, or even a border for her garden, but each stone was big enough that she was sure they would need to be moved regardless.

Even in the cool autumn day, sweat poured down Caroline's face, as well as down her sides under her dress. She could feel her lips growing chapped. It was so hot in the noon sun, in fact, that she was almost tempted to seek out the creek that Daniel had promised was just through the trees a ways. Maybe dunk her feet in.

But she already felt vulnerable out here by herself. It would never do to get lost as well.

Caroline paused and looked over her shoulder abruptly. She thought she had heard a twig break, as though under a foot. She held her breath but heard nothing more. Just the same bird calls that had rung out from high in the trees all day.

"Was that you?" Caroline called to Peanut.

The mare snorted, then resumed munching on the last of the dandelions still bravely hanging on after summer.

Shaking her head at herself, Caroline returned to her work. Though she couldn't help but listen more intently from then on, over the sounds of her own labored breathing and stones clashing against one another.

By the fourth time she'd stopped herself to listen for possible danger around her, Caroline had to admit it might be time to head back. Not only was she vulnerable out here on her own, but the more she worked the more she tired herself out, and so the less she would be able to defend herself if the worst happened.

She trickled some of her water onto her hands to clean them as best she could, then took a long drink. Wiping her bruised and dirty hands on her apron, Caroline looked around at the work she had accomplished.

"Oh, Daniel," she said with a sigh. "Where are you when I need you?"

But she knew where he was. And she knew she didn't have any right to complain. Where Caroline was healthy and capable, plenty of other people in the community were sick or old and thus needed him far more than she did. Indeed, his sense of responsibility and compassion for others was one of the things she loved most about him.

"All right," she said to Peanut as she crossed to where she waited. "I think it's time to go home. Hannah will be pleased I wasn't gone long."

But once Caroline had gotten back and returned the horse to Mr. Kirk, the first thing Hannah said when she saw her was, "Caroline, your hands!"

Caroline smiled sheepishly. "Maybe next time Daniel goes to Fort Vancouver, I'll ask him to get me some gloves."

CHAPTER TEN

Daniel returned from his journey to Fort Vancouver safely and full of stories. The new wagon was sold to the blacksmith, and Patience Sullivan got the sugar she asked for. Two days after that trip, he joined the Sullivans for supper and regaled them with descriptions of the territory. Fort Vancouver lay even farther west, on the Columbia River.

"It's enormous," he said excitedly. "Far more expansive than any of the forts we passed on the trail. Must be close to a thousand feet long."

"Goodness," Mrs. Sullivan said. "How many soldiers do they have stationed there, do you think?"

"Hard to say. I couldn't even tell you how big the barracks are. Seems like there are a couple dozen buildings inside the walls too. Not just housing and storage, but a school, a chapel, a *library*. It's incredible."

"And we thought we'd left all that behind back east," Hannah said.

"I let Dr. Martell know there's a physician there, and

Mr. Gilroy know there's a blacksmith. Miss Atkins has started making a list of books she wants for the school. Since that fort is right on the widest part of the river, just a bit inland from the bay, they're able to get shipments of supplies from the east far easier than it would be to bring them all overland. Ben and me will probably be sent out to the fort often, I'm thinking, not just for mail to send back to the states."

"It's such a blessing that we have been able to settle so near to such an important institution," Mrs. Sullivan said. "Just one day to get there and back feels downright speedy compared to so many days on the trail."

"It's bound to get slower and slower as more folks ask me to bring things back. Soon I'll have a whole new covered wagon full of supplies to drag home," he said with a laugh.

"Is that where Mr. Wheeler is getting the piano he promised Annie?" Mrs. Sullivan asked.

"What?" Caroline asked in surprise. "Really? A whole piano out here?"

Daniel shook his head. "I'm not sure. I'm not part of that at all. It might have been easier for him to have it shipped to the bigger port in San Francisco and then brought here on a wagon."

"Imagine that," Hannah said with wide, hopeful eyes. "Here I was thinking we were at the end of the world, but I suppose we could really get anything we wanted. If we had the money to pay for it."

"Which is the requirement for most things," Daniel said as he stood. "Thank you so much for supper, Mrs. Sullivan. Hannah." He tipped his hat to the two women, then turned to Caroline. "Do you mind walking me to the edge of camp?"

But she was already standing, already eager to follow him anywhere.

"Don't keep her out too late!" Junior called after them.

Caroline laughed.

"Is he going to keep doing that until you get married?" Daniel asked as he offered her his arm.

"Probably. I must hear him call himself the man of the house twice a day at least."

"Well . . ." Daniel cleared his throat and looked over his shoulder. "I wanted to talk to you about that, actually."

"About Junior? He's harmless. I'm sure he doesn't mean anything by it."

"No, not about Junior. About the wedding."

"Our wedding?" Caroline paused, instantly afraid of what he might say. "What? What is it?"

"It's nothing big." He urged her to keep walking with a gentle tug of her arm in his. "I promise I'm doing everything I can, but . . . I need to ask you to wait a little bit longer."

Caroline felt her throat tighten. She willed herself to swallow the hurt words that first sprang to mind. When she did finally speak, she couldn't keep her voice from cracking.

"Longer? Why? Is it . . . something to do with me?"

"No. Oh, my darling, not at all."

Daniel stopped walking then and turned to her. They had just passed the Waters family wagons and could still overhear some of their conversation, though with so many people talking it was impossible to make anything out. And it was unlikely they would hear Caroline as she strove to understand why this man didn't want to marry her yet.

"It is absolutely nothing to do with you, Caroline. It's just that between the breadth of tasks I am being called on to do, like going all the way to Fort Vancouver, and helping my father with his upcoming campaign for mayor of Eden Valley, I simply have not found enough spare moments to make progress on our home. With enough men, we could probably get some walls and a roof up in a week, but those same men want to be building their own homes. Everyone is spread thin. And I can't very well ask them to help me when I don't have the time to help them."

"But you *are* helping them," Caroline protested. "Why else did you take a whole day to go to the fort and back if not for every single one of the people in this town? Why don't they see that?"

"Some of them do, but carrying a letter thirty miles is quite different than giving up an entire week to build someone else's home."

"So Annie Hudson gets a house and a piano, and I get an afternoon moving rocks by myself."

Daniel stopped, his voice low. "Those two things have nothing to do with one another."

"I know," she responded, exasperated. "You're right. I'm just . . . I'm tired. And frustrated."

He sighed. "I promise, Caro, it will get done, and as quickly as I can possibly manage it. Just not as soon as we would like."

Caroline let the tears fall down her cheeks, grateful

for the twilight that would disguise such pain from Daniel. She knew it wasn't his fault, and she didn't want to make this agonizing decision any harder for him than it already was.

"I understand," she said softly. "I'm sorry. I know you're doing your best."

"Thank you." He leaned forward, pressing his forehead against hers. "I'm sorry too."

With one last sigh, Caroline resolved to move past this disappointment as quickly as she could. There was nothing else to do.

"Tell me about your father's mayoral campaign. Surely there can't be much that he needs to do, is there? Everyone in this town is here because he got us here."

"That's what I think," Daniel said. "But Pa's humility sometimes works against him. He doesn't want to take anything for granted. And then, of course, there's the fact that Pa's not running unopposed. Hugh Larson is putting his name out there as a candidate as well."

"It's surprising to me that anyone would run for mayor against your father."

"I thought the same thing, but Pa is very cavalier about it. Mama is furious that Mr. Larson would dare, but my father keeps saying that this is what democracy is all about, this is why Americans are spreading out all over the continent—the multitude of ideas, the best ones rising to the top and all that. Though, I admit, I'm not sure what kinds of ideas Larson will run on. I suppose we'll see over the next week or so."

"If nothing else, I've never heard anyone say a bad word about him. And he has that big family that seems to adore him."

"That's not enough to lead a whole new town, though."

"I know that," Caroline responded, stricken by the bitterness she heard in his tone. "I'm just trying to understand."

"Well . . ." Daniel sighed. "I'm not sure we will understand. And I'm not sure that matters. We just need to make sure we do everything we can between now and the first week of November to ensure that every man knows George Mills is their best bet for safety and prosperity, just as he has been for the last six months."

Caroline nodded emphatically.

"When is Annie Hudson marrying her beau?" she asked, trying to soak up as much time with him as she could.

"Soon, I think. I heard he was pulling up stakes and selling his farm in Dempsey so Annie could stay here with her sisters."

"Goodness, that seems quite generous. And a piano besides."

Daniel nodded. "But that also means they need to build their new home here along with everyone else. I don't know if they'll marry before that or not."

"Seems like everyone here has some collection of obstacles to get through," Caroline said, adding wryly, "Even if she *is* getting a piano."

"Yes, seems like," Daniel said, sounding defeated. "I am doing my best, Caro, but you have to understand what I'm working with here."

"I *do* understand," she insisted. "I understand everything you've been telling me. I promise I'm not trying to fight with you. I'm just wondering . . . there are forty families here, Daniel. Why are all of their problems yours?"

"They're not."

She heard the coldness and warning in his tone.

"Your father seems to have made all their problems *his*. And then yours by extension. When he is voted mayor, how much of that work is going to fall to you?"

"Are you implying that I should just abandon my father, my family, for whatever you think I should do?"

"No, I—"

"Because I thought I told you enough times, Caroline. I love you. I am going to marry you. Your safety and happiness are the most important things to me."

"That's what you keep saying," Caroline said, "but I can't help but feel like all of these other people are a priority over me. Over *us*."

"It's not like that. There's just . . . there's so much to do and so many people need my help. I thought you would understand."

She sighed. "I do. Or . . . well, I want to understand. I'm trying to understand. I guess I'm just frustrated. I'm not going to deny I'm disappointed. I suppose I just have to hide it from you better."

"Caroline, there's no need to say things like that. I don't want you to hide anything from me. If I've disappointed you, I hope you will tell me."

"Gladly," she muttered petulantly.

He paused and looked hard at her before continuing. "Is there something you would like to say to me?" he said finally.

Caroline looked up at him sharply. She had never heard such coldness in his tone. Not when speaking to her. Biting remarks jumped to mind, but she kept calm, she kept her temper. She didn't want to make anything any worse than it already was.

"No—" Her voice cracked. She cleared her throat and tried again. "No. I'm sorry, I'm just . . . it's just all hard."

"I know. But it's our responsibilities to do the best with the situations God has given us. I'm going to go back to my camp now." He paused. "You'll be all right tonight?"

She nodded. "I'm sorry."

"I'm sorry too."

And without even kissing her goodbye, Daniel strode purposefully away from her, disappearing into the darkness.

CHAPTER ELEVEN

As Caroline woke the following morning, she felt her chest tighten with anxiety before she'd even opened her eyes. She lay in her tiny cot within the Sullivans' wagon next to Hannah, trying to calm her heart as she remembered the conversation she and Daniel had the evening before.

Not conversation. Fight. It had been a fight, and Caroline felt sick at the thought.

They'd had their first fight, and even now Caroline wasn't sure where she had gone wrong. Through all their traveling, all the while grappling with lack of food and with exhaustion, and even through her wagon breaking, she and Daniel had been united as a team. But now, somehow, when she'd asked for that to continue, when she'd expressed dismay that their wedding would be delayed, she had been treated as if she were being unreasonable.

Caroline trusted Daniel. She was certain that he was doing his best for her, and maybe her own reaction had been too selfish. Now, instead, she would have to show him that she was still on his team, still supported the choices he was making, even when she was disappointed.

And so, she decided resolutely, she would do something about it. Caroline always felt better when she took action. She just hoped this was the right choice.

Accordingly, not long after breakfast with the Sullivans, Caroline tied her bonnet under her chin and made her way to the Mills family's campsite. They too still had two covered wagons, situated in an L shape around their campfire. Their camp was on the edge of the larger gathering of wagons, where families made their temporary homes as buildings went up all over town. The cattle the Millses had driven west—the ones that had survived the journey—roamed the grassy meadow around them.

Only Abby was visible when Caroline approached. She was squatting next to the remnants of the campfire, using a stick to break apart the burned-down logs and spread out the embers.

"Good morning," Caroline called.

Abby looked up, smiled, poked at the embers one last time, then stood to greet her guest.

"Good morning. Are you looking for Daniel?"

"No, I actually came to ask your parents if there was something I could help with. I figure Daniel is always so busy, there must be plenty that needs to be done."

"Just you?" Abby said. "Not, um, Hannah or Junior or anyone?"

Caroline smiled slyly at her, leaned in close, and lowered her voice. "I saw you and Junior the other night, you know. Do your parents know?"

Abby's eyes grew wide and she shook her head subtly. "Not yet," she whispered back.

"Why not? He's a Sullivan. How can they possibly object?"

"They think I'm too young for any kind of beau, no matter who it is."

"Ah, well. I don't know how you get around that except to just be patient, I guess."

"What are you girls whispering about?" came a booming voice from behind Abby.

Caroline looked up to see Mr. Mills striding across the camp toward them.

"Girl secrets," his daughter retorted. "We're not telling you."

He laughed, a warm chuckle, and turned to Caroline. "You're here bright and early. Daniel has already left for the day, I think."

"Actually, I'm here to see you, Mr. Mills. Daniel told me there's so much work to be done, with the town and with your election, that I thought . . . well, I can't go all the way to the fort like he can, but maybe you have something I can help with here?"

"You sweet child." He looked around, considering. "Why don't you find my wife and see what she is working on today? She's in charge of all this, as you can imagine, and I'm sure she'll be able to put you to work."

"Wonderful. Thank you, sir."

But he had already turned away, headed toward his horse, toward his full day of whatever it was important men did.

When Caroline turned back to Abby, the younger

woman said, "Don't tell him about Junior. Please. Or Mama. Especially don't tell Mama."

"Of course not," Caroline assured her. Inwardly, it pleased her to have been brought into Abby's confidences. "Does your brother know?"

"I don't know. I don't think so. You won't tell him either, will you?"

Caroline opened her mouth to reply but wasn't sure what to say. After some consideration she finally responded, "No, I won't tell him. It's your secret, not mine to tell. Just don't go getting me in trouble whenever he finally does find out."

"I won't." Abby squeezed her arm in gratitude.

The two women were still huddled close together when Abby's mother appeared out of one of the family's wagons.

"Abby Mills, have you started the baking like I asked you to?"

"Not yet, Mama. Caroline just got here and was wondering if there was anything she could help with."

As Abby went into their supply wagon for the ingredients and dishes she would need, Mrs. Mills's gaze fell on Caroline; her expression softened, but only just.

"Daniel has told me how much there is to do for your husband's election," Caroline began tentatively. "Is there some way you could put me to work? To help? Lighten the load, so to speak?"

Mrs. Mills raised her chin, not taking her eyes off Caroline as she considered what the younger woman had said.

A long, quiet moment fell between them. Caroline inwardly panicked that she had somehow said something wrong, but she kept silent, waiting for her future mother-in-law's response.

"Yes." Mrs. Mills brightened—almost abruptly, it seemed to Caroline. "I know just the thing. Bless you, child, for offering. What I need today is someone young and strong like you to visit every family in Eden Valley and talk to the adults."

Caroline nodded. "All right, of course. And, um, what did you want me to talk to them about?"

"I need to get a feel for their farming plans for the spring and summer. In part so George can best craft his campaign message, but also so Daniel can make whatever advanced preparations he can when he goes to Fort Vancouver again."

"Oh, yes, all right. I can do that." Caroline tried to keep her confusion out of her expression. Surely there was something more immediate or more high-value that needed to be done. But she was doing all of this to try to make up for a fight with Daniel; potentially starting another fight with his mother was far from the solution.

"I certainly do appreciate it, my dear," Mrs. Mills said in a honeyed tone.

Abby emerged then, her arms now full, and watched the two other women as she settled in next to the campfire to mix up her bread.

"Just me?" Caroline asked. "That is, you think folks will take me seriously if I show up by myself to do this?"

"I don't see why not. You are betrothed to my son, after all."

And there it was; Caroline saw it now. Though she was better at hiding her judgment, Mrs. Mills seemed to be just as protective of her son and his prospects as Mrs.

Ross had been in New York City. Both mothers looked askance at a penniless orphan seeming to depend on their sons.

So be it. Caroline would just have to work harder to show this woman her worth. Though she didn't think his mother's opinion would sway Daniel, she still did not want to enter married life with this tension.

"Of course. You're right. I'll do my best. I'm just glad there's something I can do. I know I am not as qualified as some of the others."

Mrs. Mills offered her a small smile but did not contradict her.

"All right, then," Caroline said, realizing she had better get started. "I'll do my best."

The task Mrs. Mills had set for Caroline seemed on the surface to be so easy as to be virtually useless. But after several hours of crisscrossing the town, initiating conversations and tracking down decision-makers, Caroline realized that doing this for each of the forty families, during a time when not even a single road had been established in town, was far more laborious than she had expected.

But she did it. She finished the assignment, and at the end of the day, just before the supper hour, she returned to the Mills family's camp to report her results to Mrs. Mills.

As Caroline approached the camp, she looked around and past the wagons to the cattle, hoping to spot Daniel.

"He's not back yet," Abby said when Caroline got close enough to hear her. Just as before, she was squatting next to the campfire, though the detritus around her feet showed she had been busy that day. "I think they wanted to cut down all the trees they would need for the church today, so they'll probably take all the sunlight there is."

"Goodness, yes. I imagine that's a lot."

Abby beckoned her closer. Curious, Caroline obliged.

"Did you hear," she asked in a whisper, "the pastor's wife is expecting?"

"Is she? Where did you hear that?"

"Mama doesn't realize how well I can hear," she said with a laugh. "Especially when I'm inside the wagon and she forgets I'm even there. You wouldn't believe what I've overheard."

"I'm not sure I want to know. But—really? Mrs. Montgomery?"

Abby nodded. "That's the story. So, anyway, you can see why Pa is making the church and parsonage the priority. I'm sorry it means you don't get to see Daniel today, though."

"Oh." She waved her hand, dismissing the apology. "It's fine. Really. Just being able to see your family and know that I did something to help is enough. You'll tell him I asked after him, won't you?"

"Of course."

"Miss Harper?"

Caroline turned to see Mrs. Mills standing not an arm's length away. The older woman had all but snuck up on her.

"How was everything today?"

Though startled, Caroline launched into her description of the conversations and plans that the settlers were bringing together. As she concluded, she tried to read the expression on the older woman's face.

"I hope that helps," she said, hating the desperation in her voice. "Please let me know if there's something else I can do."

"I'll do that," Mrs. Mills said. "You have a good night now."

Stunned that she hadn't even received gratitude for her day of work, Caroline quietly left. If nothing else, she could count on the Sullivans to be happy to see her.

But upon her return to the Sullivan camp, she found that supper was burning. Patience and Martha were staying out of the way, tucked under one of the wagons and practicing writing their letters in the dirt. Junior and Mrs. Sullivan were nowhere to be seen, and Hannah was wincing as she soaked her hand in a bucket of water.

"Oh, Caroline! Thank goodness."

But Caroline didn't wait to see what her friend needed. It was too clear from the smell and the liquid boiling over the top of the pot that the soup needed to be removed from the fire as soon as possible.

Catching up her skirt, petticoat, and apron, Caroline cushioned her hands with the fabric to protect them from the heat. The cast-iron Dutch oven that the Sulli-vans used for most meals would be far too hot to touch without it, as evidenced by Hannah's current state. Once she had set the pot in the dirt, she turned to her friend.

"Are you all right?" she asked Hannah, hurrying to her side.

"Yes. I just . . . I got distracted by the game the girls were playing and hadn't realized the pot had already heated through so thoroughly. I only barely touched the metal. I'll be fine in a bit."

She held her hand out to examine, and Caroline clearly saw what looked like the beginning of angry blisters on the pads of Hannah's fingers.

"How was your day?" Hannah asked, clearing trying to put on a brave face.

"Let me at least get some ointment for this."

Caroline climbed into the supply wagon for the first-aid kit and emerged to help Hannah bandage her hand.

"You were gone all day," Hannah pressed. "At least give me some good gossip."

Caroline gently dabbed at the wounds as she thought over her day. True she had talked to everyone, but none of the future plans of various families were hers to share, even if they did qualify as gossip. She thought about Abby's admitting to being courted by Junior, but then Caroline hesitated. She had promised Abby she wouldn't tell her parents or brother, but there had been no such request about Caroline not telling Junior's family. Still, she thought it better to be safe and keep the news to herself. It wasn't her secret, after all.

But then something else occurred to her.

"Well, I *did* hear something interesting . . . Do you know most of the men spent today felling trees to be used to build the church and parsonage?"

"Yes! That's where Junior's been."

Caroline checked to make sure the little girls weren't listening, then, lowering her voice, she said, "Abby Mills says it's because Mrs. Montgomery is expecting."

"Tell me everything," Hannah said, leaning forward excitedly.

CHAPTER TWELVE

When Caroline woke the next morning, she again thought of her fight with Daniel, and again thought she should do something that day to show him that she was supportive of everything he was doing. She still felt such a lack of resolution, since she hadn't spoken to him since their fight. But the idea of going from family to family again, in search of information that didn't seem to have a point, discouraged her.

She rose for the day, braiding her hair and putting on a clean dress—preparing for what, though, she didn't know.

She had tried working out at her own homestead claim, but she'd eventually been forced to acknowledge that was futile to do on her own, in addition to being dangerous. She had tried to help Mrs. Mills, but that had been both exhausting and seemingly pointless as well.

There had to be something else she could do. She could help. She was certain of it. She was smart and capable; she just needed some guidance. It might take her longer than someone else, and she might not be able to do every step on her own, but Caroline was sure that she could be of some use in her new home.

Later, as she sat around the campfire with the Sullivans finishing breakfast, Caroline put the question to them, hoping for an idea.

"What are you all doing today?" she asked. "Junior, did you men get all the trees felled you needed to yesterday?"

He bit into a biscuit and shook his head. "Close," he said around a mouthful of food. "I think they'll finish pretty early today, but I got other things I need to do." He finished chewing and swallowed. "Someone's gotta put food on this table."

"You're going out? Hunting?"

He nodded. "Lots of game still. Most of the animals probably won't be hibernating for another month yet, and I'm thinking we'll need to lay in some stores for the winter. I'm hoping to bring home enough today that we can salt and store it for at least a few weeks."

"That sounds like a lot of work."

"It will be. But I can do some today, some later this week. Little by little, hopefully we'll be set for the winter."

Caroline watched him eat for another moment before turning to the other women.

"What if I go hunting with Junior?" she suggested tentatively. "I already know how to shoot, and he could teach me the rest. Then, next time, I could go myself and free him up to do some of the heavier labor that I can't do without risking us not having the food that we need."

"Are you sure you want to?" Hannah asked, concern in her voice. "Remember, I only just talked you into learning to skin a rabbit at all."

Caroline smiled at her friend. "Yes, I know. Spoiled little rich girl. But, really. Daniel taught me to shoot. I need to get better, don't I? This could be really helpful."

"Well . . ." Mrs. Sullivan began slowly, as though she wanted to be careful with her words. "That's an idea. You know there are not many folks who would hold to a woman doing such a thing, though, don't you? There's a chance it might make more trouble than it's worth if the wrong person hears about it."

"You only have a moment to decide," Junior said as he stood and moved toward the wagon. "I'm leaving soon."

Caroline felt a pang of fear. Would it hurt Daniel if some meddlesome gossip were to learn she had gone hunting and be judgmental about it? But the specter of feeling useless and unneeded haunted her. She thought she could put up with any gossip thrown her way if it meant feeling more confident in her own abilities. Learning to hunt with Junior would accomplish both helping Caroline feel like she wasn't wasting her time and helping remove some of the pressure on the boy who was now expected to be the man of the household.

"I guess I will just have to hope that the wrong person doesn't hear about it," she finally said. "Or figure out what to do then."

Mrs. Sullivan smiled at her. "You're very sweet, Caroline. And we're very grateful to you."

She waved away the compliment and got to her feet. "Junior," she called, "are you leaving soon?"

"Yup. Just about to. Do you know where your gun is? John's gun?"

"I think so. Maybe. Give me a minute."

She climbed up into the wagon. Pushing aside the dirty canvas flaps, Caroline waited a moment for her eyes to adjust to the dim light within before she began her search.

When her own wagon axle had broken and Caroline had joined the Sullivans in their wagons, her personal belongings had been tucked into the family's storage wagon along with all of their own supplies. She had a trunk with some clothing, a couple books, and not much else; but the gun she had kept out, just in case. She found the rifle hanging from a couple pegs jutting off the wagon cover frame near the back.

When Caroline and John had left Independence, she'd trusted him to have purchased all the supplies they would need, not only for the journey but also once they reached Oregon. She'd had no idea at the time how broke he really was, how desperate their plight had truly been. Now, as she pulled down the gun and slung it over her shoulder, she realized she didn't even know if she had any extra bullets. But when she lifted the lid of her trunk, thankfully, she found a single box sitting near the top.

She climbed out of the wagon awkwardly holding the rifle and box of bullets. "Daniel showed me how to shoot, but that was . . . months ago." She paused, suddenly embarrassed. "Maybe this is a bad idea. I'll just hold you back."

"Naw," Junior said good-naturedly. "We'll give it a try. I can always go back later on my own anyway, so don't you worry about a thing." He winked, adding, "If you fail completely, no one will starve."

Caroline nodded, resolute. She could do this. She could help in this way.

He gave her a few cursory instructions—stay quiet, wait for him, keep the gun pointed down—and then led her to the stand of trees that bordered the campsite.

"We'll have to walk a bit before we get out of hearing of all the other people, and we can't talk the whole time, all right?"

Caroline nodded, still holding firm to that resolute feeling. Following closely behind Junior, she set off into the woods with her rifle held tightly in her hands. As she tried to stay as quiet as possible, she did her best to remember all the things Daniel had told her during their shooting lesson all those months ago. About squaring her hips and sighting along the barrel. That had been teaching her to shoot at a large, stationary piece of wood, and even then it took her many tries to actually hit it.

She had no idea how she would fare with a moving target, especially one as small as a bird or rabbit.

It was a good hour of walking, following Junior, before he slowed. He seemed to be listening to the woods all around them. Caroline stopped behind him and looked around, trying to understand what he was listening for.

The trees around them were a mix of different species—Caroline recognized fir and cedar, but there were several others she didn't know the names of. Unlike some of the high desert they had crossed through on their way to the Oregon Territory, this terrain was damp and lush, with moss and ferns growing up some of the tree trunks and scattered across the ground.

Junior took another few steps and then gestured to Caroline to follow. After just three steps, however, he held up a hand for her to stop. She did. Her heart was pounding. She had a million questions to ask him, but as long as he was staying silent she would too.

In keeping her eyes on Junior, she recognized the moment he spotted something. He stood even straighter and gestured Caroline to come closer. As she stepped up next to him, he extended an arm to point out a mule deer some thirty feet away.

"All right," he said, in a whisper so soft that he had to stand mere inches from her ear. "Hold as still as you can. Sight along the barrel, and when you see it move into that gap between the tree and the fern, breathe out slowly and fire on that steady exhale."

Caroline nodded, but only barely, trying to follow his first instruction of holding still. Though the deer was thankfully a larger target than the rabbit she had expected, it was nevertheless a petrifying prospect to have such an expectation placed on her.

But, she reminded herself, she had asked for this. Learning to hunt had been her idea, and if she could do this she could do anything.

The deer bent down to take another mouthful of whatever it was eating and straightened again. Caroline watched carefully. Much of the animal was blocked by the foliage, but she trusted that if she just waited like Junior suggested, her opportunity would eventually arise.

Sure enough, just moments later, the deer took two

steps forward, into the gap, seemingly unaware of the rifle trained on it.

Letting out her breath slowly, Caroline squeezed the trigger. The rifle recoiled into her shoulder, nearly knocking her off her feet. But even as she regained her balance she could hear the hooves of the deer running away.

"Did I get it?" she asked, though without much hope.

"Not this time." Junior sighed. "You know, maybe I get the next one, just to make sure that we bring home something, and then you can try again."

Caroline chuckled. "I have no objection to that plan."

Accordingly, for the next hour, she followed closely behind him, watching him carefully while also staying out of his way. Over the course of the day, they spent more time searching and listening than actually shooting at anything. He managed to kill a different deer and two quail. About midday they took a break, and Junior pulled out a canteen and jerky for them to share while he answered all her questions about what such an outing would usually be like for him.

"Pa and I used to go together once a week, back in Ohio," he said. "Started when I was maybe thirteen or so. I imagine it will be much the same here, though with so many fewer settlers we probably won't have to go quite so far from home as we did back east."

"I'm so sorry so much has fallen on your shoulders."

He smiled sadly. "Thanks. I always knew there would come a day when I was the man of the family . . . I just thought I'd have more time with my father."

Clearing his throat, Junior stood and brushed off the rear of his trousers.

"Are you ready? I think it's time for you to give it a try at least once or twice more. And then we should be getting back. I don't know how much longer I can haul around all this meat."

Soon Caroline was following him again, deeper into the woods, but this time she had at least some idea of what they were looking for, what they were listening for. He had pointed out to her some tracks left in the soft mud, and explained how animals looked for water the same way humans did. Even if she didn't end up bringing back anything, Caroline felt as though she had gotten quite the education.

Junior stopped and put his arm out to stop her. Her eyes raked over the landscape in front of them, but she didn't see anything until he pointed it out specifically.

A small, light-brown rabbit, blending in almost seamlessly among the dirt and tree trunks it had surrounded itself with. The rabbit was alert, looking around, but from this distance Caroline didn't think it could sense them.

"Your turn," Junior whispered.

She wanted to protest—it was too small, it was too far away! But this was what she had come for in the first place.

Aiming her rifle, she anchored her feet and squared her hips. The weapon was heavy, but she had a firm grip. She ran through all the things Junior had told her and, finally, just lifted up a prayer. It couldn't hurt, right?

Keeping her eye on the rabbit, Caroline squeezed the trigger.

CHAPTER THIRTEEN

The rifle recoiled into Caroline's shoulder. Half a dozen birds flew up out of the foliage all around them, escaping the loud noise. From this distance, Caroline couldn't see where the rabbit had gone, but the low fern right next to where it had been quivered.

"Did I get it?" she whispered.

"You did!" Junior seemed almost as surprised as she was about it. "That's a good meal for six people, Caroline. That's really something to be proud of."

"I did it? Really? I—" She choked out a laugh. "I did it!"

Junior laughed too. "And now let's collect your victory and go home. This deer is getting too heavy for me."

He turned away from her to fiddle with something in his pack, so Caroline was left to find the game on her own. It was at least twenty feet away, but she knew exactly which tree it had been near. She stepped carefully over the roots of nearby trees and approached. The animal had been just over a foot long, not counting the ears, and was now stretched on its side in the dirt. The fur wasn't nearly as bloody as she had expected, and though she had never expected such a task would be a part of her life, Caroline did not hesitate. She squatted and picked up the creature by the ears.

The next thing she would have to learn was how to skin it, something that John had pestered her to do before he died and that she had only just promised Hannah she would learn.

With a deep breath, Caroline returned to Junior. She took on part of his load; she could easily carry the bag and the two birds along with her rabbit. She would need to work to get the blood stain off of her apron and the cuff of her sleeve, but that was a small price to pay for the sense of pride and accomplishment she felt.

Their walk through the woods back to the camp was far quicker, given that they didn't bother to stay quiet. Junior kept the conversation lively asking Caroline questions about New York City.

"Is it true that you all had to get water from upstate? Pa told me there are no wells in New York City, but I just can't imagine that."

"I certainly never saw any wells while I lived there. It's an island, you know, so a well might not be that stable."

"Is it?" He looked at her with wide eyes. "So, then, there are bridges and things to get to the mainland? Or did you have to take a boat to get to America?"

Caroline laughed. "I think a lot of folks who live in Manhattan forget it's not part of the mainland, but yes, there are lots of bridges."

The pair finally emerged from the woods late in the afternoon. As they walked through the scattered campground, between the wagons and the families they had traveled west with, Caroline got the distinct impression that all eyes were on her. She raised her chin, just a little, in defiance. Who cared if she had blood on her apron, or was carrying game? Plenty of women in the territories had to do far more. She resolved not to think about it, but kept her gaze ahead until they reached the Sullivans' campsite.

"Caroline Harper!" Hannah stood from where she had been scrubbing the little girls' dresses against the washboard and gaped at her. "Did you do it? You really did it?"

"Just this one," she said modestly, holding up the rabbit. "And I needed plenty of help."

"You shot *that*?" Hannah asked in wonder, before laughing incredulously. "You clever girl! I never would have been brave enough to even try, and yet you went with no hesitation and returned a success."

"Barely. And there was plenty of hesitation, believe me." Once she'd relieved herself of her burden, Caroline all but collapsed into the grass at the edge of their camp. She stretched her legs out in front of her, leaning back on her hands. "I might need to throw this apron out."

"I'll see what I can do with that stain," Hannah said. "But first, let's deal with the spoils of battle."

Caroline laughed. "Please tell me it will be easier next time."

"It will be easier next time. But, do you want there to be a next time? I'm sure we can find another option. This doesn't have to be your job."

"You know, I don't think I mind, really. It's . . . well, it's not easy, and it's not pretty, and I'm sure I look a fright, but there is a certain sense of accomplishment in bringing home supper. Somehow it feels much more tangible than just doing the laundry again."

"We'll see how long that thrill of victory lasts," Hannah said, laughing. "I'm sure there's a reason Junior has been able to fill his days with so many other things."

"You're probably right. But for now, at least, it is nice to feel like I'm helping in some material way."

"She did great," Junior called. He was exiting the wagon, carrying a whole leather roll of the knives and tools he would need to skin and butcher the game they had brought back. "Just needs some practice."

"A *lot* of practice," Caroline clarified, pulling herself up from the ground to help.

As Junior started skinning the animals, occasionally giving her tips and instructions, Caroline launched into her story about the day she had spent tramping around the woods. Hannah was a rapt audience, asking questions and wide-eyed as she listened.

"And even though I couldn't hit the much larger target of the mule deer," Caroline finished, "somehow— I don't know how—I managed to hit the rabbit. I can't imagine it ever happening again."

"Just needs practice," Junior said again. "You can go out with me again when I go, but you gotta carry your own kills."

"That seems fair."

"I gotta say," Hannah remarked. "Remember back when I very first met you, at that campsite outside Independence?"

"And I was wearing a silk dress and didn't know how to do a blessed thing? Don't remind me."

"All right then." Hannah grinned and turned her attention back to her laundry. "All I'm saying is that girl is long gone."

Caroline warmed under the praise. "Do you need help with that?"

"You're not too tired after your long day of providing for the family?"

"Very funny. I'll heat you some more water."

Caroline got to her feet, but before she could even pick up a bucket, Abby Mills approached their camp. She seemed to be more timid than Caroline had ever seen her.

"Are you all right, Abby?"

"Yes, thank you. I was just sent over to check if Junior will be available tomorrow for the construction team. It looks like you all were busy elsewhere today."

She peered over Caroline's shoulder to where the young man worked furiously. If Caroline didn't know better, she might suspect Junior was so focused on his task that he had no idea they had a guest. But she had been living side by side with the young man for months now, and to her experienced eye it was clear that he was sitting up a little straighter, holding his knife with more grace, and had even angled his body a bit more toward Caroline and Abby's conversation.

"Did you want to talk to him about it?" Caroline asked, trying to keep her tone casual.

"Only if you think it won't be interrupting him."

She leaned in to whisper to the younger girl, since

none of the rest of the Sullivans knew their secret. "I'll keep the others busy as long as I can."

Abby blushed and shook her head subtly.

"Go ahead," Caroline said in a normal volume. She gestured toward where Junior had set up his work in the space where the Sullivans' two wagons came together.

As Abby passed the rest of the family, intent on speaking to Junior, Hannah shot Caroline a puzzled look.

With a shrug, Caroline lowered her voice and said, "Oh, you know, Mrs. Mills always needing information about everyone else, I suppose."

In a louder voice, trying to make it clear that she was not trying to eavesdrop, Caroline began asking detailed questions about the laundry she was to be helping Hannah with—how each stain would be treated, and what she should do about the blood on her apron. Each was answered carefully, though clearly Hannah was a bit confused why it seemed as though Caroline was putting on such a performance.

Fortunately, Abby didn't stay long, and in fact left the Sullivans' camp without much more than a wave goodbye to the rest of the family.

As soon as the younger girl was out of earshot, Hannah turned to Caroline.

"What under the canopy was that?"

Caroline tried to hide her smile. "I haven't the faintest idea what you mean."

"What? You have to tell me! You can't act like your head is full of air, when I know very well it is not, and then not at least explain what that was all about."

Hannah laughed, but the incredulity in her expression was unmistakable.

Caroline glanced over her shoulder at Junior, who was again focused on the work ahead of him, but without the self-conscious posturing of before.

"It's not my secret, so you can't tell a soul, but . . . Abby and Junior are courting," Caroline finally whispered.

Hannah's mouth hung open in shock. She let out one sharp laugh, then turned to look at her brother.

"Don't say anything," Caroline warned her. "Abby doesn't want anyone to know. I probably shouldn't have even told you."

"Why doesn't she want anyone to know? She's not embarrassed by my brother, is she?"

"Oh, no. I think she's smitten, to be honest. But her parents think she is too young to be interested in anyone, even Junior Sullivan."

Hannah pursed her lips. "Well . . . they're not wrong. Sixteen is very young, but I know lots of other folks don't think so."

Both women looked back at Junior again.

"He has so much on his shoulders already," Hannah said in a soft voice. "I hope he's not thinking about taking on a wife too."

"Time will tell," Caroline answered.

CHAPTER FOURTEEN

Not every day dawned that Caroline needed to find or create some way that she could be helpful. Just a handful of days after she had gone hunting with Junior, the weather was so bad that not a soul in their small community attempted to get any work done. The campsites were a mire of mud and puddles, and the intermittent rain interrupted anything the settlers might attempt to do.

All of that made it perfect timing for a wedding.

After traveling all the way west from Virginia to answer the call for a mail-order bride, Annie Hudson finally married Isaac Wheeler on a chilly day in late October. The weather was wet and cold enough to halt much of the construction work that had been in progress throughout Eden Valley. A hopeful celebration was the perfect alternative.

As Isaac had already lived in Oregon Territory for a year, he had the resources and energy to build them a home faster than the other men. Several of Isaac's friends from Dempsey had traveled to Eden Valley and stayed for a week to help him, pooling together their supplies and putting all their efforts into a place that Annie could call home. The Hudson sisters, not unlike the Sullivans, had no man of the family beyond Isaac, and he took his responsibility seriously.

"Do you know where they built their place?" Caroline asked Hannah as they picked their way through the mud to where the wedding would be held.

Though Pastor Montgomery's church had been made a priority, it still wasn't much more than cleared land and a growing stack of logs; nevertheless, it was the best place for the entire town to gather. Luckily, in the days leading up to the ceremony, Annie had seemed absolutely unperturbed by the prospect of being wed in a construction site.

"I think nearer to the mountains on the north side," Hannah said. "Closer to Dempsey. Mr. Wheeler must be quite the generous man to give up everything he had already built there to start over again here."

Caroline nodded. "Daniel has talked to him a little. Says he seems like a good man. And he must be, to take on the rest of the Hudson family too. That certainly was not part of his original agreement."

"Well . . . a lot has changed between the eastern states and here, that's for certain."

The two women had almost made their way to the church site when Daniel and Benjamin hurried up to meet them, each offering their own arm to their respective betrothed and together escorting them the rest of the way. As Caroline walked carefully so as not to slip in the mud, she mourned the state of her boots and the hem of her dress, already damp with the light showers they'd had to walk through.

This was the first time she'd had more than a quick hello and goodbye with Daniel since their fight, but he seemed to have put it behind him. Maybe he'd heard about how hard she was trying, or maybe he'd simply cooled his temper. Whatever it was, Caroline was happy to also put it behind her. They walked hand in hand to the crowd gathered at the church site, sharing news of their weeks as they went.

The wedding itself was simple but heartfelt, even more so with so many of Annie's fellow emigrants gathered to watch. Caroline looked on with a conflicted heart. She didn't want to be envious; she knew she had plenty herself to be grateful for. She knew without a doubt that Daniel was doing his absolute best for her. But that didn't mean she couldn't wish it were her own wedding day.

But even as she had that thought, Caroline recognized the futility of it. Even if she and Daniel were wed that day, where would they go? And for that matter, how would they even get there? Borrow another horse and ride separately out to nothing more than an open field?

Annie Hudson, on the other hand, would wed her farmer, climb into the wagon he had built the previous summer behind the two horses he had purchased months earlier, and be whisked away to a home built with the love and support of men who would always be there to help in the future.

Caroline sighed deeply.

"Are you all right?" Daniel whispered.

The pastor was still speaking over the couple,

extolling the virtues of patience and understanding in any marriage.

Caroline nodded, then smiled at him.

She would have her groom and her home in time. There was just work and waiting to get through before then.

There was no celebration planned for after the wedding ceremony. The bride and groom went off to their new home while everyone else dispersed to try to stay out of the rain as best they could. Daniel and Benjamin walked the women back to the Sullivans' camp before returning to their own commitments.

"How was it?" Mrs. Sullivan asked as they approached to walk back to camp with her too. "Mrs. Stephens just passed on her way to her own camp and said the groom seemed incredulous at his own luck."

Daniel chuckled. "That's the perfect way to put it. I don't think he took his eyes off her face once."

"Even when he was trying to put on the ring," Hannah chimed in.

"That's wonderful," Mrs. Sullivan said. "That poor girl has been through so much. She deserves to be happy."

Again that pang of envy stung Caroline, but she pushed it down and turned cheerfully to Daniel. "What is it you boys have to do this afternoon?"

"Fishing."

She grimaced. "Now? In this weather?"

He looked up at the sky glowering down at them. "I think it's clearing up. But, even so, people gotta eat. And just like everything else, we only have a few more weeks until real cold weather sets in. There's still so much to do. I really shouldn't have taken a break for that wedding, but I thought you would like it if I was there."

"I did. Thank you." Her mind whirled, thinking about when she could get Junior to take her hunting again. If Daniel didn't have time for a break, then neither did she. "Would you like help?"

"With the fishing? Oh, no, Caro. I wouldn't want you waiting out there with us. Especially if I'm wrong and it does start raining again."

"No, not to wait. To fish. You could teach me to fish, couldn't you?"

He stopped walking, guiding her out of the path of the others that had been following behind them. As the small crowd of people passed on their way to their own camps, Daniel looked intently at Caroline.

"Where did you get this idea of wanting to fish?"

"Where did I get the idea?" Caroline frowned. "I don't know what you mean. You just told me it's something that needs to be done, and I want to be able to help however I can, and . . . Do you not want me there? Is that it? I'm not trying to argue with you, but—"

"It's not that I don't want you there, it's just . . ." He looked away and ran a hand through his hair in frustration. "Caroline, I want you to believe—to *know*—that I can take care of you."

"Of course I do, but—"

"And that means that I will make sure you have a home and plenty of food and pretty dresses and whatever else. You don't need to be standing ankle-deep in a river trying to catch something for supper as long as I'm alive."

"Daniel, I *know*," she insisted. "I'm sorry. I didn't

mean to imply I doubted your ability to provide for me. But I see how hard you're working and how stretched thin you are, and I just wish there was a way for me to take some of that burden from you. I can help. Please let me."

He seemed to relax at that.

"All right. Thank you. Okay." He nodded over and over. "I didn't mean . . . Thank you, Caro. I'm sorry."

"You have a lot right now, Daniel," she said softly, leaning into him. "But I'm here. I can help, can't I?"

"Not fishing in this weather, no." He grinned at her. "But we'll find something. I promise. I know you want to help, and it must be frustrating to not be able to see the kind of progress you have been hoping for."

"Especially seeing other women get married," she teased.

He smiled softly. "I'm sorry."

"But please do let me know how I can help. Please."

"Today, I would like you to stay safe and warm and not get sick like Ben and me are apt to." He offered her his arm again so they could continue the walk back to the camp. "And I promise to keep thinking about it. Everything that comes to mind, like the labor to clear our homestead, or the money we need to buy the food and supplies we can't gather ourselves, isn't something that you can solve for me. But I'll keep thinking. I promise."

"Thank you."

They walked on in silence for another few minutes, each lost in their own thoughts. Caroline didn't want to overstep. The last thing she was trying to do was make Daniel feel as though she didn't trust him to take care of them. At the same time, it hurt her so much to just feel idle while he raced from one side of the territory to the other, always pressed for time, always exhausting himself.

It would be a miracle if he didn't end up sick himself soon.

They arrived at the Sullivan campsite, where they said goodbye.

"Be safe," Caroline said to Daniel as he kissed her cheek.

With a grim smile and a wave, Daniel headed toward his own family's campsite, where presumably he would gather all the supplies and gear he would need to spend the rest of the afternoon fishing. Caroline looked up at the sky. It was still a dark, overcast day, but it wasn't actively raining. Maybe Daniel was right; maybe everything would be fine.

"How do you want to spend the rest of your day?" Hannah asked. She looked up at the thick clouds herself. "If it doesn't rain."

Caroline smiled. "I was thinking I might go hunting."

CHAPTER FIFTEEN

"Miss Harper, a word, please. Mrs. Hatchley tells me that you were spotted last week covered in blood, dragging the body of some dead animal behind you as you emerged from the woods."

Mrs. Mills had appeared at the Sullivans' campsite as though from nowhere, bearing down on Caroline, who blinked at her in surprise at the picture painted.

"Well. Um. That's not at all how I would have characterized the situation."

Caroline and Hannah had been spending all afternoon heating water for the Sullivan family. It had been at least a couple weeks since the little girls had had a proper bath, and Caroline thought it might have been even longer for Mrs. Sullivan. Hauling bucket after bucket of water from the river was a chore in and of itself, but heating enough water—and keeping it hot—and then heating more as each family member took their turn, was enough to fill their entire day.

Wisps of hair had escaped from Caroline's braid and

were sticking to her face with the sweat. She would take her turn last, and so had spent much of the day bent over the fire, keeping it lit and removing the heated water to take it to the large washtub.

"Oh no?" Mrs. Mills's arms were crossed tightly over her chest. "She also led me to believe that you had gone out into the woods unchaperoned with an unmarried man."

"I'm sorry—what?"

Caroline was too shocked by such an accusation to even come up with a response. She had been so used to staying silent and compliant with Daniel's mother that now, when she was confronted directly, she was at an absolute loss.

"I won't have you shaming my son—my family—with your inappropriate behavior."

Mrs. Mills had raised her voice by now, attracting the attention of the rest of the Sullivan family. Caroline looked around at the nearby camps, wondering if any of the other families could hear this confrontation, and how long it might take them to spread it around the entire town.

Mrs. Sullivan approached the two women cautiously. "Mrs. Mills? June? I'm sorry, is there something wrong? Let me help, if I can."

Caroline unconsciously took a step back, away from the attacks, away from the anger and vitriol. Her mind whirred as she tried to make sense of what Daniel's mother was saying. Her confusion blocked out the rest of the conversation—Mrs. Mills indignantly explaining to Mrs. Sullivan, while the latter tried to gently calm her down.

Caroline rubbed her face hard, trying to focus, trying to understand what she was dealing with. The last time she had spoken to Mrs. Mills had been when she reported the results of her full day of effort on behalf of the woman's husband. How had they gotten from that to this? She stepped away from the campfire and closer to the upset woman.

"I will not have my son be made a fool of," Mrs. Mills declared.

"Nobody thinks that," Mrs. Sullivan said soothingly. "Caroline is like one of the family. Junior thinks of her as a sister. It is no different than if he had taken Hannah hunting."

"Well." Mrs. Mills looked at Caroline, then Hannah, and back to Mrs. Sullivan. Caroline could see the moment when she mentally chose to back down from that particular objection, recognizing its futility. "Still, the very idea of a woman hunting is positively . . ." She spluttered, unable to come up with a word bad enough for what she meant. Finally, she settled on "Unacceptable!"

"June," Mrs. Sullivan said, stepping closer. "Everyone is being asked to do things they never thought they would. Why, my own daughter had to lead a team of oxen for part of our journey. And somewhere I heard that Abby was making braided rugs to sell and help raise money. Surely you don't begrudge Caroline for doing her part?"

Before Mrs. Mills could respond, she was interrupted by the appearance of Daniel in the midst of the Sullivan camp. Caroline's heart lifted—he would explain; he would defend her.

"Mama? Is something wrong? Abby told me she saw you storming off . . ."

Daniel trailed off as he took in the women gathered, their expressions and stances. He fell back a half step. "What's happened?"

"Your— This—" She pointed at Caroline. "I have been advised that Miss Harper went hunting last week unchaperoned with Junior Sullivan. I have been further advised that she went hunting *on her own* in the days after that. She does not seem to have any appreciation for how that might reflect back on our family."

Caroline took a deep breath, trying to keep her temper. Daniel's expression revealed nothing, but if Mrs. Sullivan was willing to defend her, Caroline knew she couldn't have done anything too terrible.

"Mrs. Mills," she ventured. "I'm so sorry. I didn't— I don't—" Caroline shook her head, unable to find the right words. All of her training for New York society and what would be proper for a young woman of her standing was utterly useless in this scenario, and she felt adrift. "I'm sorry," she said again.

"I think, Mama," Daniel said, glancing at Caroline, "that she recognizes how much she has upset you. She's sorry. It's in the past, and . . . can we just let it go? I'll talk to you about it more tonight."

Mrs. Mills huffed, looking at all the rest in turn.

"No one appreciates my position," she mumbled, then turned to go.

They all watched Mrs. Mills walk away, shoulders square as she proudly bore her disappointment and shame all the way home. Mrs. Sullivan squeezed Caroline's hand in comfort, but then tugged Hannah away, leaving the couple to have a private conversation.

Caroline turned to him cautiously, as though he were a skittish cat.

"Daniel, I'm sorry. I didn't think—"

"I thought I told you that I would take care of us." He didn't turn to her, but stayed facing the fire, avoiding her gaze. He sounded defeated, exhausted. "Why did you do this? Were you just looking to attract my mother's ire?"

"No!" she protested. "This wasn't about you, Daniel. I have other people to whom I am responsible. Junior can't do everything for this family, so I offered to learn so I could help more. So Junior could be free to do other things—"

"Like maybe help build our house soon," Daniel suggested.

"Well—but—" she stuttered. Caroline felt wrong-footed. How were so many of her best intentions being misinterpreted? "Yes, sure. Or the church or the general store or a house for the Buchanans or . . . Daniel, I'm sorry, it didn't occur to me that my actually contributing to this community in a meaningful way would be such a problem. What do you want me to do?"

"I want you to trust me. I want you to be patient like I've asked of you so many times."

"I am, Daniel, but I can't very well just sit and wait for you to have time for me."

"I thought you understood that I have a lot of demands on my time, Caroline."

She flinched at the use of her full name; he hadn't called her anything but *Caro* or *darling* in weeks, it seemed. Feeling tears well up in her eyes, Caroline thought over how little time he had had for her since they had arrived in Oregon; she thought over how much he was trying to accomplish, seemingly all on his own. She felt a pang of shame, thinking over how useless she had felt before she had asked Junior to teach her how to hunt. And now he was trying to take that away from her?

"Daniel, I honestly don't know what you expect me to do. I can't just sit on my hands, properly quiet, waiting for you to notice me."

"Just . . ." He shook his head and looked into the distance over her shoulder as though looking for the right words. "Just be like everyone else, Caroline."

She was too hurt to respond, but her mouth hung open. He pulled her into a quick hug, whispering into her hair, "I'll see you . . . soon. A few days, maybe."

And then, before she'd recovered her ability to speak, he was gone.

Caroline watched him go, aware of the tears spilling down her cheeks, but made no effort to wipe them away.

"Caroline?" Hannah put a gentle hand on her arm. "Are you all right?"

Turning and throwing her arms around her best friend, Caroline let out all the hurt sobs that she had been holding in while Daniel had been there.

"It's okay," Hannah said, hugging her tight. "You're all right. Tell me all about it. It's okay."

Caroline tried to catch her breath. She tried to forget the look on Daniel's face when he told her to be like everyone else. She tried to ignore the hurt that kept pushing her sobs to the surface.

"Let's get you a bath," Hannah said, carefully

detaching herself. "I've been heating some clean water, and you can have the next bath. It'll be just what you need. Come on."

Caroline allowed herself to be led toward the wagons, where blankets were strung up to offer some semblance of privacy, even as they were living in the literal dirt. It didn't seem as though a bath would solve anything, but she had nothing else to try.

CHAPTER SIXTEEN

Caroline went to bed early that night, citing a headache. Even the littlest Sullivan girls were still awake, playing with cornhusk dolls, when Caroline climbed into the sleeping wagon. She took down her hair and rubbed at her scalp where the pins had been digging all day.

How had she gotten to this place where she and Daniel were fighting over what seemed to her such an unnecessary concern? Did he really want her to be like everyone else? Rather than the paradise she had expected when they reached the Oregon Territory, it seemed like everything had just gotten more difficult since they'd arrived.

She turned over onto her side, so her face was almost right up against the canvas that stretched over the top of the wagon. It had the earthy smell of the trail, the dirt and campfire smoke in which she had lived for the last seven months, bringing back memories of April—such a faraway time, it felt now—when she saw her own covered wagon for the first time and the dismay that had accompanied that.

She had started out, back in Missouri, refusing to bend from the east coast expectations she had been raised in. It took work and failure, but little by little Caroline had learned how to take care of herself, what was truly important, and how to find her place in this new world. It seemed as though it was only when she stopped trying to obey all the societal expectations that she had finally felt like herself.

And now Daniel was trying to take that from her.

But, on the other hand, Daniel loved her. He only ever wanted the best for her. He had helped her so much when she was so close to losing everything. Maybe she was the one being unreasonable.

Caroline tossed and turned, trying to fall asleep lying on one side and then another, but always with her mind an anxious blur of hurt and confusion.

Even though she had gone to bed early, Caroline didn't fall asleep for ever so long. She kept her eyes closed tightly when Patience and Martha came to bed, listening to the little girls giggle and whisper until their breathing slowed. She kept her face turned away when Hannah and her mother came to bed later, hoping that neither of the women could guess that she was still awake. Outside the wagon cover, the sounds of animals lowing and campfires being smothered followed as, little by little, the entire campground fell asleep. It seemed that only Caroline was left awake, contemplating how she could fix the mess in which she had inadvertently found herself.

The cold in Daniel's voice had chilled her. Caroline did not know what she would do if she lost him.

She had no intention of finding out.

She would just have to try harder. She would have to try again. She would have to dampen her immediate instincts and try to always make sure she was making the choice that "everyone else" would make in her shoes.

Caroline wasn't entirely sure how she would be able to do that, but with this tentative plan in place she was finally able to fall asleep shortly after midnight. When she woke the next morning, she was the only one left in the wagon; all the Sullivans had risen long ago.

She felt like an old boot—worn out, dirty, at risk of being discarded. Caroline tried to invigorate herself, stretching as she sat in her cot and then combing out her braid. Her auburn hair spilled around her shoulders, clean from her bath the previous afternoon. As she ran her fingers through her hair, delicately pulling loose any knots, Caroline thought over what she had decided to do that day.

She wouldn't go hunting. She wouldn't go out to the site of her future home. She wouldn't wear trousers or chew tobacco or go to Fort Vancouver or do anything else that Mrs. Mills might disapprove of. No, Caroline Harper would shrink herself down, contort herself into whatever shape she had to in order to not cause a fight. Maybe sometime in their married future she and Daniel could talk over this problem again, but right now the thing he needed most was for her to not add to his list of problems to deal with.

She just hoped she could figure out how to do that.

By the time Caroline finally freshened herself for the

day and climbed out of the wagon, the Sullivans had already finished their breakfast.

"Hey, darlin'," Hannah said gently, handing Caroline a cup of coffee. "How're you feeling this morning? You slept a lot."

"I didn't fall asleep until late." She sighed. "It was a rough night."

Caroline was grateful her voice hadn't cracked; she was hesitant to say more, lest she cry.

"Do you want to talk about it?"

Caroline offered her friend a bright, though not completely sincere, smile. "No. Thank you. I think I'd rather just get to work."

Hannah smiled back. "You should eat something though. You skipped supper last night."

"Are there any biscuits or johnnycakes I can just take with me?"

"Take with you? Where are you off to?"

"I thought, if she has such a strong opinion about how I should be spending my time, then maybe I should just offer myself to Mrs. Mills to be put to work."

Upon hearing the bitterness in Caroline's tone, Hannah's smile fell.

"I don't mean—" Caroline began. "I just thought . . . well, you know, surely if Daniel is always so busy there must be something that I can do to help, you would think. Right?"

"Right, but . . . Caroline, didn't you try this already? You offered your day to Mrs. Mills and she had you gossiping about plans that might never see the light of day. Is that really the best way to spend your time?"

"I don't know what else I'm supposed to do."

She heaved a sigh and looked down into her cup of coffee.

After a long silence, Hannah finally said, "I don't know either."

Caroline took a long sip of the coffee as she watched the action in the campsite all around her. So many of the families had men and boys who had spent weeks now clearing land, felling trees, planing lumber, and the like, all as best they could with the tools they had. The Jamesons had almost completed a one-room cabin where all five men and boys would sleep. The Waterses were halfway done with two cabins, even with Colin and Nancy leaving to settle elsewhere in the territory. The church had a floor and most of all four walls. Sean Gilroy's blacksmith forge was little more than an organized stack of stones around a fire, but it was progress.

All the Sullivans had was Junior, who was only sixteen years old. They would have to wait for more men to be freed up from their own families' responsibilities to help.

All Caroline had was Daniel.

With a final resolved sigh, Caroline drank down the last of the coffee, grateful for the bit of sugar Daniel had been able to bring them from the fort. It was yet one more reminder of how he loved her and took care of her. She took the cold biscuit Hannah offered and stood to go.

"I'll see you for supper?" Hannah asked as Caroline began to walk away.

"Let's hope so."

This late in the morning, many of the wagons and campfires Caroline passed seemed quiet, some of them virtually abandoned, as man, woman, and child headed off into the countryside to build their homes or forage for resources.

There were dozens of children—too young to be of much help though. Little girls like Patience and Martha Sullivan or Kate Keegan were kept busy collecting sticks to feed into campfires. Caroline knew that Miss Atkins was still holding classes for the smaller children—more frequently now that the whole town was camped in one place—but she thought that was on the far side of the camp. The consensus was none of the older children would be going to school until the following fall, as they were needed for labor in the meantime, so the school itself would not be built by the town until the spring.

As she approached the Mills family's wagons, it was clear at a glance that Daniel was nowhere nearby; his horse was gone too. It was also abundantly clear, from the look on her face, that Mrs. Mills was none too happy to see Caroline. When she was still thirty feet away, Caroline almost slowed her steps. She could feel the hostility and doubt from here, and she almost turned around. But then she spotted Abby. She thought about how this was the family she wanted. This was the sister she could have if she just figured out how to make everyone accept her.

Reminding herself why she was subjecting herself to this humility and uncertainty, Caroline continued forward.

"Can I help you?" Mrs. Mills said, not coldly but seemingly without interest in her answer.

Caroline cleared her throat and watched her feet as

she closed the distance between herself and the other woman.

"I, um . . ." She looked up at her. "I wanted to apologize. Again. I didn't intend . . ." She trailed off, not wanting to start another fight. "I wanted to offer myself, too, for whatever you might need. Or your husband. Or the town. Or . . . I'd like to help. Please."

It was that final *please* that softened Mrs. Mills. Caroline regretted not having thought in advance about what she was going to say, but in the end her sincerity and humility won the day.

"Abby!" Mrs. Mills called over her shoulder. "Come show Miss Harper what you're doing for Pa's campaign."

"Thank you," Caroline said as the younger girl hurried over.

CHAPTER SEVENTEEN

"Oh, good!" Abby exclaimed upon hearing that Caroline had come to their camp to offer help. She rushed over to greet her. "You'll be perfect! I'm so glad you're here to help me." She seized Caroline's arm and led her toward the Mills family's wagons, away from her mother and the possibility of being overheard.

"What are we doing?"

"I'll show you." She pulled Caroline past the wagons, around to the other side, which stretched into a grassy meadow where the family's cattle grazed. Abby looked back around the corner, as though afraid they had been followed. When she turned back to Caroline, she had a mischievous gleam in her eye.

"Is this a secret?" Caroline asked in a whisper.

"Yes! I want to see Junior today, but I didn't know how I was going to get away from my mother. But then you just showed up—it's perfect!"

"I don't understand."

"You'll cover for me, won't you, Caroline?"

"You mean . . . lie? To your mother? Absolutely not!"

"Not *lie*. Just . . . make sure our assignment is completed, even if I'm not there. That's all she'll ask about anyway. I never would have been able to do it all on my own and make time for him, but now you can help."

"Abby, no. Why are you putting me in this position? You know the last thing I want to do is upset your mother more."

"You won't. I promise. She is so thrilled you're here now to volunteer, she won't even think about anything else."

"She is?" Caroline tried to peek around the corner of the wagon at Mrs. Mills.

"Of course!"

Caroline peered back at Abby, unsure how strictly truthful the younger woman was being. But she didn't have any grounds to object. No matter what her other motives, Abby had far more knowledge of her mother than Caroline herself did.

"Don't you want to help get your father elected?"

Abby shrugged. "Sure. I guess. But Mama has this idea of me charming all the men into voting our way, and that just doesn't sound like me, does it? I'm much better off spending my time with Junior."

"It feels like you're just setting me up to disappoint your mother."

"No! It's not like that. What I'm saying is, she will probably be disappointed either way, so we both might as well get what we can out of it."

Caroline groaned. "Abby . . ."

"Please," she begged. "Wouldn't you go out of your way to see Daniel more if you could?"

Caroline sighed, admitting to herself that Abby was probably right. And, anyway, she was doing what she set out to do—help Mrs. Mills and prove her worth in no small part so she could see Daniel more.

She shook her head. "I still don't like this."

"Just come with me. Walk with me to where I'm meeting Junior, and if you still don't want to, I'll just say hello and then we can go."

Caroline groaned again, but found herself nodding. "Fine. But don't forget you still haven't even told me what we are actually supposed to be doing for your mother today."

"Oh, that's easy." Abby waved a dismissive hand as she reached into her family's wagon, withdrawing two large baskets. "She wants us to talk to all the men who can vote."

"I did that a week or so ago. What's different this time?"

Caroline had accepted one of the baskets from Abby, and now she chanced a peek under the homespun towel that had been wrapped and placed over its contents. Even just pulling aside a small corner, she could smell the warm, welcoming scent of cinnamon. Placed inside in neat rows were several dozen small, fresh doughnuts.

Her eyes widened. "Doughnuts?"

"Just, you know . . . hospitality." Abby shrugged with a grin.

"We're bribing people for their vote?"

"Oh, no!" Abby seemed genuinely shocked. "No, we'll give one of these to whoever we meet, no matter their vote. There should be enough. It's more of a . . . Mama calls it an opener. A reason to start a conversation with someone. We go to each campsite, offer whoever is there a cinnamon doughnut, and then steer the conversation to the election."

Caroline grimaced. "I can't believe this is what your mother wants us to do. After all her complaints about my hunting not being ladylike . . ."

"It's different. It's just talking. Come on. I'll show you."

With the other basket handle slung over her own arm, Abby led the way through the Millses' campsite, waving goodbye to her mother as they went, and crossed the small distance to the wagons set up next to them in the meadow. Just like where the Millses had made their home, their close friends the Findleys had positioned their two wagons at an angle to each other, making a wall against the expanse of the territory, and had cleared grass for their campfire near where the two met.

"The Findleys?" Caroline asked in a whisper. "You really think that Mr. Findley needs to be convinced to vote for your pa?"

"We're just practicing," Abby whispered back. "Besides, Mama says we can't take anything for granted."

"Hello, girls," Mrs. Findley said, standing at their approach. "If you're looking for Ben, he's out helping put the floor in for the church in town."

"Oh, well, that's too bad. You see, my mother and I made these"—she held out the basket—"and we're going around making sure people get to try them. Is Mr. Findley here?"

"No, dear, I'm sorry. He's meeting with the blacksmith and Mr. Emerson to discuss more building plans. Can I help you with something?"

"Well, take a doughnut anyway," Abby said, offering her basket. "And be sure you tell Ben and Mr. Findley what they missed."

"That's mighty sweet of you."

Caroline couldn't help but think Mrs. Findley seemed suspicious, watching them carefully as though knowing there was an ulterior motive.

"Is my father not at the same meeting?" Abby asked. "You know that he's aiming to be elected mayor next week. I would have thought he'd want to keep an eye on everything he can."

"No, I don't think he's there," she responded, breaking off a piece of her chosen doughnut. She took a small bite, and her eyes widened in surprise. "This is incredible!"

"Oh, good! I'll tell Mama you said so. Do you happen to know if your husband was planning on voting for Pa?"

Mrs. Findley smiled knowingly. "You know, his vote is so certain there hasn't even been a need for him to tell me specifically. Of course he's going to vote for your father."

"Oh, that's so good to hear. Well, I suppose since none of the rest of the family is around to try a doughnut, we should be going. Lovely to see you, Mrs. Findley."

With a friendly grin, Abby led them away. Caroline had not said a single word throughout the interaction and was at a loss for how she could handle the next one, especially if Abby wouldn't be alongside her.

"That was incredibly awkward," Caroline said in a

whisper when they were far enough away. "It's transparent and forward. How am I supposed to do all that naturally?"

But her concern was dismissed.

"All right," Abby said, excitedly. "Now that you know what Mama wants us to do, we'll just walk over to say hi to Junior, and then you can decide if you want to just take care of the rest of the canvassing on your own."

"Abby . . ."

"He's not that far. Come with me."

"Someone is going to see us!"

Abby led her out of the general campsite, down the narrow road toward where the bulk of the town was being built. Caroline looked over her shoulder, terrified they were being watched or followed. She had no idea how she would explain what they were doing if someone were to ask. When she posited this concern to Abby, the younger woman just shrugged it away.

"As long as you look like you know where you're going, no one will stop you."

"I don't even want to know how you know that."

Just before the girls reached the spot by the river that had been cleared for the general store, Abby made an abrupt right turn, leading Caroline to a stand of trees not far off the river's edge. In the bright morning light, Junior Sullivan was seen plainly waiting amongst the trees, though Caroline realized that with the shadows and the angle from the road, he would only be noticed if someone knew to look for him.

"Why—uh—Caroline!" he spluttered as they approached. "This is, um, a surprise. What are you all doing here?"

"She knows," Abby said.

He looked from one to the other. "She does?"

Caroline nodded wearily. "I do not like keeping secrets."

"But you will, won't you? You promised." Abby stepped closer to Junior, as though allying herself with him against Caroline. "You won't tell anyone, right, Caroline?"

"I—" She looked helplessly from one bashful face to the other. She didn't want to be pulled into this secret. She didn't want to give Abby's mother any more reason to disapprove of her. But what could she do? She wasn't about to tell the couple's secret either. "Fine," she answered dejectedly. "Don't make me regret this."

"Thank you! I swear, we're just going to talk. In fact, we'll probably stay right here—"

"Maybe don't tell me details," Caroline said, taking a step back. "The less I know, the less I have to lie about."

"You're not going to have to lie," Abby said. "We'll just tell Mama we split up and you lost track of me. But you should probably take both baskets. Just in case."

"Abby . . ." Caroline groaned. "Please don't do this. Please just come back with me and finish this thing that your mother wants you to do."

"It'll be perfectly fine." Abby's tone was airy, but with a steel behind it that Caroline recognized from Daniel. There would be no changing her mind.

"I'll take care of her," Junior said. "I don't have all day, either. It's just for a little . . . Thank you, Caroline."

She took the second basket from Abby, and before she had even moved away more than a few feet, the two lovebirds were huddled close, giggling and whispering together. Caroline felt a pang of loneliness, missing Daniel, missing the closeness that they'd had in the past.

But as she followed the road back to the campsite, she reminded herself that this errand that she was spending all day doing would be in service of regaining that closeness. This was something she could do for his family. For her new family. And though she felt embarrassed to do it and frustrated with Abby for leaving it all to her, there was no doubt in Caroline's mind that she could do it—and well. After all, what Mrs. Mills wanted her to do was not all that different from the delicate courting and gossip conversations she had participated in back in New York City's parlors. There was the subtlety of what was unsaid and the understanding of everyone present. And now, at least, she even had the gift of fresh doughnuts to help ease herself into the conversation.

Abby would make her own mess, and it was clear that Caroline was not going to be able to talk her out of any of it.

As she approached the campsite, the closest wagon was that of the Robinson family. Caroline squared her shoulders, put on her brightest smile, and confidently approached.

CHAPTER EIGHTEEN

The vote for mayor of Eden Valley was drawing closer, and as it did, it seemed as though the two candidates—George Mills and Hugh Larson—were in competition to see who could sleep the least, who could be in the most places at once, talking to the most men and making the biggest impression. Otis Van Anda had initially thrown his hat into the ring for consideration as well, but had quickly dropped out when he saw what was required to be a contender. He was already losing too much sleep with a newborn baby in his wagon.

After her day spent giving out cinnamon doughnuts and spreading the word for Mr. Mills, Caroline found herself even more invested in the election than she had expected to be. She wished she could vote herself, but since she couldn't, she looked for other ways she could contribute.

This vote was taken more seriously than anything Caroline had seen on her journey thus far, and for good reason. This would decide not only who would lead their fledgling community, but for how long.

When he had last visited Fort Vancouver, Daniel had brought back a sheaf of paper and a dozen pencils to be used for this and any future voting. At first, Mrs. Mills had vowed that she would protect those ballots with honor and dedication, before her son had talked sense into her. He managed to convince her such single-mind-edness could potentially open her up to accusations of impropriety should her husband win.

And June Mills valued what was right, good, and proper above all else.

Instead, Pastor Montgomery had volunteered to hold the precious materials until the day of the election. He and his wife spent an afternoon watching over Caroline, Amy Cole, and Sadie Waters, the three of whom had gathered to make the blank sheets into the necessary ballots.

"I've done the math," Amy said as she pulled the stack of blank paper toward her. "I figure we need to make one ballot for each man—"

"And each family," Sadie interjected.

Amy bowed in acknowledgment, then barreled on. "Each family, plus ten percent in case of damage, errors, lost, or other unforeseen circumstances."

"Have you done something like this before?" Caroline asked, looking at the fourteen-year-old in confused awe.

"No. But I read a lot."

Sadie chuckled. She was a bit older than Caroline, and had come west with her husband and his entire family, including five siblings and another spouse. The

Waterses were a big family, and very popular among the wagon company. Though Caroline hadn't spent much time with them, she wasn't sure she had heard anyone say a bad word about any member of that family.

The three young women were seated on the newly finished plank floor of the yet-to-be-named Eden Valley church. There were no walls yet, and no furniture, but progress was being made, and they were perfectly capable of writing out the ballots on the floor as not. Besides, it kept them up out of the mud that was becoming more and more prevalent as the weather cooled.

"You girls need anything? You'll do all right here if I go pray with Mrs. Buchanan?"

Caroline looked up to where Pastor Montgomery stood just off the floor platform, where the steps up into the church would eventually be. Mrs. Buchanan waited a bit past him, trying to look as though she wasn't listening.

"We're just going to walk to the river"—he pointed—"so if you need me you can just holler."

"Thank you, Pastor," Caroline answered. "We'll be just fine."

"But you should probably check our work when we're done," Amy added. "We need to be sure this is all above reproach. Miss Harper is going to be marrying into the Mills family, after all."

Sadie chuckled again. "Amy, are you friends with my husband's sister? She's about your age, I think. Faith? There's something about you that I think she would just love."

"All right, then," the pastor said pleasantly. "I'll be back soon."

Caroline watched him go, and then looked back at the two young women who she would be with the rest of the afternoon. Someone needed to take charge of the entire enterprise, and she wasn't sure that the fourteen-year-old—despite her confidence—was the best choice.

"All right, then," she began. Caroline cleared her throat and tried to instill a sense of authority into her tone. "So we're clear, I just want to reiterate that we are here to create the blank ballots for the men to vote for who they would like to be the first mayor of Eden Valley."

Sadie offered a playful applause.

"I think the most efficient, but still thorough, way to do so would be to create a spot on each ballot for Mr. Mills, for Mr. Larson, and then a blank where men can write in a name if they choose."

"You think someone is going to write a name other than those two?" Sadie asked.

"I have no idea. But it's best if we don't make any assumptions."

"I think that's very smart," Amy said, nodding seriously.

"Thank you." Caroline reached for the stack of blank paper in front of Amy and lifted off the top section. "How many men did you say there were, Amy?"

"There are forty families, but several of those families have more than one man of voting age. Like the Hatchleys or"—she nodded at Sadie—"the Waterses."

"Then we should probably make . . . seventy or eighty ballots or so, just in case there is an error or someone drops his in the mud or something. Let's say seventy-five. That comes to twenty-five for each of us, and then I thought we could check each other's to make sure there's no confusion nor any . . . extraneous marks."

"No way we can be accused of cheating," Amy supplied.

"Precisely. The last thing any of us needs is a question around the legitimacy of this election."

The three young women got to work, each hunched over their stack of paper, carefully writing out the required words as clearly as they could. After a few moments of silence, they seemed to fall into a rhythm. Caroline was conscientious about the clarity of her printing, while also trying to put just as much effort into each name so there was no question of favoritism.

"How close is your husband to having your home built?" she asked Sadie as they worked. "I imagine with all those brothers it should go pretty quickly."

Sadie looked up at her, smiled, and focused back on her work as she answered. "Well, you know, they're all mama's boys to some extent, so the cabin for his folks was finished a couple days ago. They all made that a priority. Angus and I don't mind, of course. But that means that they're not starting on my house until today."

"That's wonderful for you, though. You'll be home soon enough."

"Our house already has a floor," Amy interjected. "The men won't let me help, but the doctor is."

"Dr. Martell is letting you help with what?" Caroline asked.

"Help him treat all the injuries. Well, I guess there

are not as many as there could be, but some of the boys aren't being as careful as they should."

Sadie and Caroline exchanged glances of alarm.

"Did something happen?" Sadie asked. "I hadn't heard."

"Let's see . . ." Amy sat back and began counting on her fingers. "Mr. Jones sprained a finger. One of the Mr. Davises sprained a wrist. Mr. McKinnon has bruised ribs. And . . . what was the fourth one? Oh! Jefferson Clark dislocated his shoulder." She shivered dramatically, as though the memory were too gruesome for words. "That one was rough."

Caroline paled. "And to think I was disappointed that I couldn't help with the construction."

Sadie shook her head in wonder. "I'll be having words with my Angus, I think," she said with a grim grin. "I'd better not be hearing about any broken bones or misplaced shoulders."

"Dislocated," Amy corrected her.

"I know, Amy," Sadie said, her grin widening. "I was joking."

"Oh." Amy looked mildly confused, before turning her attention back to the ballots in front of her.

The young women worked silently for another few minutes before Amy spoke up again.

"Are either of you interested in purchasing a braided rag rug?"

Both Caroline and Sadie paused as they looked at the younger girl.

"To buy," Amy clarified, seeing their confused expressions. "For your homes. For the floor."

"We know what a braided rug is," Caroline said with a smile. "Are you selling them?"

"Abby Mills is. I think she has three or four done, but no customers. My sister tried to tell her that most folks make their own rag rugs, but Abby was insistent. You don't know anyone else who might want to buy one from her, do you? I told her I would ask."

Sadie shook her head. "Why does she want to sell these rugs? Can't her family use them?"

Amy shrugged. "She just keeps saying that she wants to be able to save up money."

"That's strange," Sadie murmured, turning to Caroline. "Surely her father will support her until she's married, right?"

"Of course." Caroline dismissed any suggestion that Abby actually was in need of financial help. There must be something else going on here, though she wasn't sure she understood her future sister well enough to ferret out what it might be. "But I think Abby has far too much energy to use up every day. She's a lot like her brother in that way."

Sadie laughed. "One of Angus's brothers is like that. The world needs all kinds, I'm sure."

As the girls finished up the ballots, Caroline's mind kept going back to Abby's strange behavior. Her questions about Caroline starting a shipping business, her secrecy around her relationship with Junior, her dismissiveness about her mother's opinion.

If only Daniel could be around more. She needed to speak to him about his sister. Something was going on there, and she was at a loss what it could be.

CHAPTER NINETEEN

After days and nights of constant canvassing, after Caroline was certain she had spoken to each man in the town at least half a dozen times, after she and Abby had fried and given away what must have been hundreds of doughnuts, all their work was finally being put to the test. The first week of November arrived and with it the inaugural election day for the new settlement of Eden Valley.

Pastor Montgomery oversaw the voting in the half-built church, as the most trusted man in the settlement. He and his wife handed out the ballots Caroline had helped prepare, and they made sure that each man had a pencil and no questions. Voting took place from just after midday through to just before suppertime, with each man coming all the way to the church when he could find a moment in his afternoon. The pastor and Miss Atkins, the town's teacher, counted the ballots as they came in.

While their men decided the future of their frontier

town, the women of Eden Valley kept themselves busy making the wild settlement more of a home. Mrs. Mills and Mrs. Findley had organized a kind of potluck celebration for the evening. After the ballots had all been counted, the new mayor would be announced and the town would come together sharing in food and music to honor the new leader. Caroline in particular tried to distract herself from the voting by cleaning everything she could think to clean, from the little girls' aprons to the wide wagon seat that had been sitting out in the elements for months. She was only partly successful; the wagon needed more help than she could manage. She and the Sullivans had planned on bringing freshly baked bread to share at the official announcement gathering, but even several loaves of that couldn't fill her entire afternoon.

"I just feel like this will be the beginning of the end of all the nonsense. To be honest, I'm not entirely sure I care that much who wins," she told Hannah as the two women kneaded. "At the very least, this one big project will be behind us. Daniel's father won't be spending so much time trying to talk folks into voting for him, and then Daniel won't have to cover so much of what his father could do instead, and then hopefully we'll be able to start progress on our house . . . and *then* we can finally get married." She heaved a sigh.

"And you can leave me forever."

Caroline scoffed. "You know that is not even close to what is happening! At this rate Ben will be finished building your house long before Daniel is finished with ours, and then *you* will be the one leaving *me* forever."

"Oh! And maybe if Daniel's father *is* elected mayor,

he can ask favors and send some of the other men to help Daniel."

"Do you think there's a chance he won't be elected?"

Hannah shook her head. "No, not really. It would be very surprising if Mr. Larson won. Not impossible, but I would be shocked."

"Me too," Caroline murmured.

It was only a few hours later that they learned the truth. Just as the pioneers had gathered near the center of their future town to learn what their settlement would be named, so too did they gather at suppertime to hear the results of their first election. The tall ponderosa pine towered, lifting the spirits of all who saw it.

Samuel Findley held a folded piece of paper tightly in his fist as he climbed onto a nearby tree stump and raised his hands for quiet.

"I'm not one for speeches, as you probably know. And my wife tells me that there's food over yonder getting cold, so I'll not talk any longer than I need to. Thank you to everyone who helped make this happen. I'm sure there are too many for me to name."

"Who won?" a voice called out from the back of the crowd. Caroline and others turned to look, but there was too much laughing and jostling to be sure who had spoken up.

"Yes, all right." Mr. Findley smiled, cleared his throat, took a deep breath, and unfolded the paper, reading it over carefully before finally speaking. "The first mayor of Eden Valley, Oregon Territory, is Mr. George Mills. Congratulations, sir!"

But his well-wishes were lost in the cheer that went up. Caroline was elated—she had helped make that happen. But it was even more encouraging knowing that her new home, this little town that was becoming so much part of her heart, would be so well looked-after. Mr. Mills was lost in a crowd of men who wanted to congratulate him directly, and Caroline fell back to where a small group of women were organizing the supper for the gathering.

That night, Eden Valley held what could only be described as a party. Mr. Larson was a very gracious loser; he had spent the entire day smoking venison to share around with the community whether he won or not. He seemed just as genial in his loss as he would have been with a victory. Martin Jameson and his fellow musicians set up for a night of dancing, and Josie Hudson had pooled all the resources she could beg and collect to bake a cake, albeit small, complete with a light coat of icing. Isaac Wheeler had driven his wagon over, and as there was nothing in the town remotely resembling a table just yet, that's where all the women had deposited their shared dishes of bacon, beans, rolls, rice, and whatever stewed vegetables Daniel had been able to bring back from the fort.

Caroline and Hannah had made several fresh loaves of sourdough, with a thick crust that should pair perfectly with the soups that Mrs. Sullivan and Mrs. Hatchley had made. Caroline was proud to have contributed, though as always felt like she should be able to do more.

As the crowd broke up after the announcement, streaming out to find a seat, collect food, or congratulate the new mayor, Caroline found herself near Mrs. Mills, overlooking the gathering.

"Wonderful turnout," Caroline said. Though she didn't expect effusive gratitude for how she had contributed to the mayor's campaign, she did hope that maybe things with Daniel's mother could at least be less standoffish.

"Oh, I wish we'd had more time," Mrs. Mills said, looking around at the cleared patch of land where the town was gathered. "I just know this could all be more festive, and I don't want folks to think we didn't care."

Caroline looked, too, but didn't see what the other woman saw. To her eyes, it was an open space full of happy people who didn't seem to ask for anything else.

"Everyone seems happy enough," she said.

"Hmm."

Caroline looked around for Abby, though she didn't want to draw attention to her absence by commenting on it. Maybe the younger woman was with her father.

Or brother. Where had Daniel gotten to? She knew he must have voted, but she hadn't seen him yet.

The band started playing then, and any more earnest conversation seemed pointless. Everyone was having a good time, and whatever expectations Mrs. Mills had put on herself were hers alone to bear.

"Can I bring you anything?" Caroline asked before she went to get her own supper.

Mrs. Mills shook her head while still looking around, almost not acknowledging Caroline at all.

Well, thought Caroline, she had tried. She made her way to the line of folks waiting to get food. Carrying her plate and utensils all the way to the clearing where the gathering was being held had felt awkward, but now, as her stomach rumbled, she wished she had gotten in line earlier. Hannah and Ben sat close together on the river-bank, oblivious to anyone but each other. Abby was still nowhere to be seen, but neither was Junior.

Isaac and Annie Wheeler slipped into line behind her.

"Newlyweds!" Caroline said, though she felt a particular pang at being alone in the queue without her own betrothed. "How is your honeymoon?"

"Oh . . ." Annie blushed and smiled at her husband. "About what you would expect for a frontier town, I think. No marble floors or European tours."

"You did get a new dress though," Isaac pointed out in a teasing tone.

Annie looked down at herself and smoothed the skirt of her navy-blue dress. It looked warm and service-able—exactly the thing she would most need for the upcoming winter.

"It's lovely," Caroline said.

"Thank you. It's more than I needed, but my husband insisted."

Caroline felt a pang of longing when she saw the way Annie smiled at Isaac. She looked around again for Daniel.

"Don't go getting used to all these gifts, wife," Isaac said teasingly. "We've got to settle into real life sooner or later."

As they continued to tease each other and banter behind her, Caroline finally reached the front of the line, where she was able to fill her plate and bowls with food. Everything smelled good, each dish crafted with the care, work, and practical tastes of the pioneers. No home in New York that Caroline had ever been to would offer such primitive fare, and yet she knew that this simple food would taste better than any four-course meal she had eaten back east.

Clutching her plate piled high with the offerings of her neighbors, Caroline looked around at the gathering that spread out across the grass. Everyone seemed occupied, and nowhere did she see Daniel. Sadie and her husband, Angus, were still in line for food. She finally spotted Abby, who was hovering with a group of girlfriends near her parents, but who kept looking over her shoulder, presumably for Junior. Caroline's stomach growled as she smelled the warm gravy that drenched her biscuit. She needed to find a place to eat.

There was plenty of room next to Hannah in the grass by the river. Her friend would forgive her for interrupting alone time with her beau. Caroline made her way over to the couple.

"Can I sit with you?" she asked as she stood over them.

Hannah looked up at her. "Of course! Sit, sit."

"Don't let me interrupt."

"Nonsense."

Caroline made herself comfortable in the grass next to Hannah. Ben continued on the topic they had been discussing when she'd arrived.

"I'll take you there sometime. The fort. It's bigger than you'd ever think, and the shipments they get in! Some of them have come all the way from New York City. The trappers send out their pelts and get in all kinds of luxuries. Soon the territories will be just as populated and civilized as the states back east."

Caroline remembered some of the gilded and

papered parlors she had been in and wondered if she would see the same here. She kept eating, not interrupting.

"Here she is."

Caroline turned to see the tall figure of Daniel Mills standing over her. She all but dropped her plate and utensils in her rush to scramble to her feet and embrace him.

"Daniel!"

She threw her arms around his neck as he swept her off her feet.

"My darling girl," he murmured into her hair. "I've missed you."

He set her on her feet once more and she took a step back to look at him.

"I've missed you too."

Caroline basked in the warmth of her beloved's smile, just as the warmth of the sun sank below the horizon, setting on this new chapter for the small frontier settlement. Everything finally felt right again.

CHAPTER TWENTY

"Have you eaten?" Caroline asked Daniel.

He had appeared by her side as if from nowhere while everyone else was finishing up their supper. She hadn't seen him for several days and felt like she had no idea what was going on with him or how he had been spending his time.

"I have. A little. I'm sure there will be some left over still later. I just wanted to see you first."

"Thank you," she said breathlessly.

"Do you want to walk with me?" he asked meaningfully. The look in his eyes made her think of previous walks they had taken after sunset, alone in the moonlight, several nights while crossing on the Oregon Trail. This time, though, he held a lit lamp.

"Yes, please."

Their connection had been so fragmented as of late, with as busy as Daniel had been. All Caroline could do was be available when he had time for her. She left her plate with Hannah and went with him.

Without another word, he took her hand and guided her through the crowd. As they went, he waved to the handful of men who shouted their hellos; Daniel seemed just as popular in this small community as his father was. Caroline felt so fortunate to be by his side; he could easily succeed his father as the mayor of Eden Valley in a few years.

"Congratulations on your father's election. I'm so proud of him," Caroline said. "You must be so proud too. He has worked so hard . . ."

"I am, yes."

"And now he's the mayor of a brand new town. It's incredible to think about what he's done. What we've *all* done."

They left the gathering behind and walked longer in silence into the darkening night, but Caroline barely noticed. Her thoughts had turned to her own father, and what kind of man he might have been. She'd been only ten years old when her parents drowned at sea on a voyage home from Europe, and her brother had become her guardian. But even before his death, Caroline had few memories of her father. He had been a widely known and impressive man even beyond the city, leading a ship-building company, and with all the social prestige that came with such a remarkable business. She had vague memories of peeking through the stair rails as her parents left for an evening out, dressed to the nines after accepting one of the myriad of social invitations they received weekly. In his own way, Joseph Harper must have been a leader.

But seeing how Daniel's father had stepped up to the uncertainty and demands of leading a community on the frontier inspired an admiration in Caroline that she had not felt before. It reflected well on his son; she was marrying a man with integrity and strength.

They had left the crowd behind, the lively music fading. It was getting dark fast, and Caroline huddled closer to Daniel and the relative safety of the circle of light emitting from the lantern.

He still hadn't spoken, and Caroline now grew concerned. Had she done something wrong? Was his mother again complaining about her behavior? She cleared her throat, electing to dive into the potential storm rather than wait for the worst.

"Now that the election is over and your father is the mayor, do you think more of our energy can be directed to building our house? So we could get married? Please? I would just love if you had a warm bed to come home to after another long trip to Fort Vancouver."

She didn't want to have to beg. It pained Caroline to plead with him, to put her desires so plainly, but she felt as though she had no other options.

Daniel sighed. "That's what I wanted to talk to you about."

"What?" she responded in a whisper, hoping against hope that he would have good news for her. For them. For their future. She cleared her throat and tried to steel herself. "What is it?"

"First, I promise you that we *will* get married. There's no need to worry that it won't happen."

"All right," she responded warily.

"I know that this is what we were working toward, but there's still so much more to do. We had hoped the church would be completed by now, for example, and

Ben and I have to make more trips to the fort. And . . . I'm sorry. The last thing I want is to disappoint you, but we need to be realistic."

Caroline had stopped walking by then, stunned by the realization that her hopes had been dashed yet again. She had spent the last week telling herself that she was doing everything she could, that they both were, that they were so close to the end, and now it seemed like that was all for naught.

"But . . . ?"

Daniel stopped too. He turned back and looked down at her with a pained expression. The flickering lamp threw up shadows across his face, making him look almost unfamiliar. Where was her love, her beau, her champion who she was supposed to be building a life with?

He did not answer her implied question, so she pushed forward, the panic inside of her rising. "What am I supposed to do, Daniel? How long am I supposed to wait with my life upended?"

"The Sullivans are happy to have you."

"The Sullivans barely have enough to care for themselves. That's why I tried to learn how to hunt, remember? Before your mother put a stop to that. There is already far too much being asked of Junior already, and I am just one more mouth to feed."

"Hannah will be married soon—"

"Oh, yes, *Hannah* will be married. Of course. Why is it that Ben Findley can find time to build their home and you cannot? I honestly do not understand. I am doing literally everything I can do—everything your mother approves of, at least—and still it seems we are no closer."

"Caroline, I'm sorry. I don't know how many times we have to have the same conversation. I am doing my best."

Though he didn't raise his voice, she could clearly hear his frustration in his tone.

"I'm doing my best too," she insisted, "but somehow that's not good enough. Not for your mother, at least, and maybe not for you either."

He looked stricken. "Why would you say that?"

"Daniel, please. You know perfectly well your mother looks down on me. For a whole host of reasons, and I'm sure I don't even know them all. And given how reticent you seem to be about my being involved in the building of our life together, I can't help but wonder if you feel the same way."

He clenched his teeth; she saw the muscle in his jaw tighten and wondered if she had taken it too far. She took a small step back, reassessing.

"I'm sorry," she said, more gently. "I'm just tired and frustrated. The same as you."

He nodded slowly, but wouldn't look at her.

"Daniel," she continued. "I'm strong, and smart, and capable. Maybe hunting is not the most ladylike of excursions for me, but . . ." She threw up her hands hopelessly. "It needs to be done, and I can do it. We're not in those eastern cities anymore. We can't be precious about what is and is not proper for a young lady, and I don't know how to explain that to your mother. I don't know how to explain to you that I am willing to do whatever it takes now. No one thought it was unladylike when I was driving a team of oxen west after my brother died—why are things different now?

We have so much ahead of us, and I want . . ." She trailed off, unsure how else she could convince him.

"I know, Caro. I do. Mama is just worried about you," he mumbled.

"You know that's not the case."

"Caroline, I really don't have time to mediate between you and my mother. This is something you're going to have to deal with. We all have our crosses to bear, and mine is getting everything done that needs to be done before snow falls. I can't do that if I have to worry about your feelings being hurt. There is far too much else pressing."

"Including building a home for you and me," Caroline added pointedly.

"Yes, and if I can, I absolutely will."

She felt as though her legs might collapse underneath her. "Wait . . . it's 'if' now? *If* you can? Daniel, what are you saying?"

He stopped and took a breath before saying anything more. Caroline was grateful for the pause. She could feel her own temper flaring, and fighting with Daniel was the last thing she wanted to do.

"Do you want me to walk you to your camp, or back to the party?" he said wearily, looking around. Mrs. Keegan and her two small children had just passed them on the trail on their way back to the campsite. "It sounds like most people are still there, but it's getting late."

She didn't take her eyes off of him. "I want you to answer my question. I need to know what is expected of me. Please. Do you still want to marry me?"

"Of course I do." He sounded exhausted. "I wish

things didn't have to be this way, but we both knew when we set off for the Oregon Territory that settling in a whole new place would be a lot of work. I just need you to continue to be patient and understand that I am trying to get through the work as best I can. I hope you can do that."

"I *am* patient," she said sullenly. "I am being patient. I have been patient for weeks. But what am I supposed to do while I'm being patient?"

He shook his head. "I don't know, Caroline. Ask Mrs. Sullivan. Ask my mother. I'm sure there is plenty that needs to be done, but I can't hold your hand every step of the way. The only way I am going to get ahead enough is if I am not worrying about you every minute."

He wasn't intending to be cruel; Caroline heard exhaustion in his tone, not pointedness. But all the same, she flinched at his words. The idea that in her frustration she was becoming a burden to him broke her heart.

"I understand," she said softly. "I'm sorry. I'll do better. I'm sorry."

"I'm sorry too."

He pulled her into a hug, and she buried her face in his chest with arms wrapped around his waist. She clung tightly; he was her anchor in this storm. Even if things were unsettled between them, Caroline didn't know to whom else she could turn. Whatever she did next she would need to do by herself.

"Will you walk me to the wagons, please?" she asked meekly.

"Of course." He kissed the top of her head and

squeezed her in a quick hug before pulling away again. "Thank you for understanding, Caro."

She smiled at him, though she trusted the relative darkness to hide the sorrow she was sure was clear in her eyes.

"We're both doing all we can," she said.

CHAPTER TWENTY-ONE

Without the looming goal of the mayoral election, and without having any firmer idea of when she would be wed than she had before—perhaps even less firm now—Caroline spent the next several days feeling unmoored and uncertain. Daniel had been her anchor, and without his reassurances, everything that she had been counting on was up in the air. She no longer even trusted her own judgment for what she should do next. Daniel had urged her to be patient, but it felt as though everything she had tried to fill her time with while being patient was the wrong choice.

Instead, Caroline woke each morning and went through the motions of the chores and tasks that helped the Sullivan family, but she couldn't rouse herself to do anything more. She found no interest in reading the books she had brought from back east. She felt like she had no energy to seek out Daniel, to dream about their future, or to even take initiative of any kind. Though she thought vaguely about attempting to hunt for the family's meals again, she didn't have the energy to handle whatever consequences and arguments that might come as a result.

It was as though Caroline had been defeated in a game she hadn't realized she was playing. After all the struggle and fighting she had gone through just to survive this long to get to Oregon, now she wondered what it all was for. She had not felt so low since she had been ripped away from everything she had in New York. With no warning at all, her brother had all but dragged her away from the city and her previous life in it. At least now she didn't feel quite so much like she was starting over from scratch.

After the third day of Caroline not even showing interest in spending the morning reading to the smallest Sullivan girls, Hannah finally spoke up.

"Come with me," she said with authority, holding out her hand for Caroline to take.

They had just finished breakfast, Caroline drying the dishes before putting them away; Mrs. Sullivan was sitting down with the little girls to practice their letters. Hannah tugged on Caroline's hand, pulling her to standing from where she had been leaning against the back of the wagon.

"Grab a bucket. We're collecting water."

Caroline didn't even show a glimmer of curiosity about what they were collecting water for. To her, it seemed as though every day was the same. This was just one more item on the same list of chores they cycled through over and over. Of course they would need to collect water. They had to collect water every day, some more than others. Why not now?

With no objection, Caroline picked up two of the family's buckets and followed after her friend through the chilly morning.

The town of Eden Valley was being established on either side of a modest river that flowed west from the mountains of Oregon to the Pacific Ocean. The wagons and temporary campsites had spread out on the north bank downstream from where the rest of the town was being built. Hannah and Caroline made their way between a few of the wagons to the edge of the water. After some of the long, dry stretches of the Oregon Trail, it was a blessing to not have to travel far to collect their water, since it usually required several trips.

Low bushes grew in patches along the river, and the girls made their way between two of them. Once they were alone, out of earshot of any overeager busybodies who might also be at the river's edge, Hannah put down her buckets and turned to face Caroline head-on. She put a hand on either shoulder.

"What?" Caroline asked with a frown.

"You can't keep on like this."

"Like what?"

"I can't pretend I know what you're going through," Hannah continued, looking her friend deep in the eyes, "but I do need you to know that I'm here if you want to talk about any of it. You don't have to struggle through whatever you're feeling alone. We've been through this all before, remember?" She grinned. "You're a mite stubborn, Caroline Harper, thinking you have to do everything by yourself. But you're part of a family now, and families support each other."

Caroline offered a weak smile, tempered by the tears that filled her eyes. "Thank you."

"Sit." Hannah gestured to the grassy bank.

"I thought we needed to collect water?"

Hannah laughed as she sat right where she had been standing. "We do. We will. It can wait a few minutes for this."

Caroline sat next to her friend and pulled her knees up, wrapping her arms around them and looking straight out over the water to the other side. From this vantage, the mostly finished church and beginnings of the general store were too far upstream to see, but in the distance she could spot the clearings and slowly growing stacks of logs where three other homes were being built. All around them families were getting settled and lives were getting started, while Caroline continued to collect water in someone else's buckets.

"It's been a few days since the election, but you've been mopey that whole time. When's the last time you saw Daniel?"

"Yesterday. Only briefly. He just had time to say hello and goodbye quickly when he returned again from Fort Vancouver."

"They've had him going all the way out there quite a lot, haven't they?"

Caroline nodded. "I know his father trusts him completely, and I imagine there are only so many unattached men"—her voice cracked at this—"who that can be said about. I understand."

"But it's okay to be disappointed," Hannah said gently. "None of this is easy."

Caroline nodded, but she didn't trust herself to speak.

Hannah put a hand on her arm and squeezed lightly.

The two women sat quietly for another few minutes, each lost in their own thoughts.

"I'm just . . . I'm tired. And I think . . . I think I give up," Caroline said finally.

Hannah looked alarmed. "What do you mean, you 'give up'? After all you've gone through to get here?"

"It's too hard. The waiting and being patient is difficult enough, but even once we're married that won't be the end of it. If I can't make Daniel's mother happy, then the rest of my life with that family is going to be impossible."

"I'm sure we can figure out something. She's not unreasonable . . ."

Caroline gave her friend a flat look.

"She's not!" Hannah insisted. "She's just . . . particular."

"Yes, well. I don't know how much I can keep trying to make that *particular* woman approve of me. There has to be a better way for me to spend my time. I don't see the point in giving that woman another minute. And then Daniel will grow tired of me. And then I'll just be alone out here in the territories."

"I'm so sorry," Hannah said softly. "You must be so frustrated."

"Do you have any kind of similar problems with Ben's parents?"

Hannah shook her head apologetically. "No. They're not terribly involved, but they're supportive."

Caroline nodded and looked back out across the

water. A bit upstream from where they sat, a large boulder was situated in the middle of the river. It was so big, in fact, that even as the water rushed around it, the very top of the boulder stayed dry, seemingly unaffected by the cascading current around it.

Her options, Caroline thought, were to be like the boulder or be like the water. She could be stubborn, pretending that nothing around her was changing, and be slowly worn down against her will. Or she could just let go. She could do her best with what she had and keep going.

She sighed and got to her feet. "Well, sitting here all day isn't going to find me any answers, I suppose. We should get back."

Hannah stood as well, and the two quickly and carefully filled their buckets and returned to the camp.

"You know," Hannah began as they walked back, "Mrs. Mills has that temperance society she is trying to start. And I seem to remember hearing that she wanted to get a sewing circle— No, a quilting circle started. Maybe you could help her with one of those. Maybe it would help her see you as the kind of public-focused, responsible woman she wants for her son."

"Maybe . . . but do you really think that just checking off a list of tasks will work? I'm sure she's had servants before, Hannah, and I don't particularly care to be lumped in with that category in her mind."

"No, that's true . . . Let's hope that's not how she treats daughters."

Caroline had a flash of Abby Mills in her mind, remembering how the younger woman displayed a backbone and a streak of independence that Caroline herself did not.

Or had not, at least, in a while.

They reached the Sullivans' camp and Caroline set down her full buckets of water by the front wheel of one of the wagons.

"What are we doing with all this?" she asked.

Hannah shrugged. "I don't know. I just wanted to get you moving and talking to me."

Caroline stared at her friend a minute, stunned, before bursting out laughing. "You are too good to me, Hannah Sullivan."

She winked. "You know there's always laundry to do."

Caroline groaned.

"But I'm sure we can use this water for plenty of other things too," Hannah finished.

"Of course," she said with a tired smile. "Always more chores. Always something. I'm tired."

"I know. I'm sorry."

"I don't know what else I'm supposed to do," Caroline said dejectedly. "What more could I possibly give that family to show them I am serious, that I'm worthy of being one of them? It goes so much deeper than just performing the tasks she wants me to."

"Caroline, there is nothing you need to do to prove that you are worthy of Daniel's love."

"Tell that to his mother."

Hannah pursed her lips. "I will. If you think that will work."

Caroline smiled sadly. "Thank you, but no . . . I don't think Mrs. Mills would take kindly to anyone disagreeing with her too baldly."

"Oh, goodness, once I heard Abby tell her mother that if she wanted a daughter who was more compliant she should have had more children." Hannah laughed at the recollection.

Caroline paused and looked at her friend, an idea forming in her mind.

"I have an idea," she said. "It's the only thing I can think of left to try."

"Do you want to tell me about it?" Hannah suggested. "Maybe I can help."

"No." She stood. "I think I would rather wait to see if it works. Then you can either praise my genius or comfort my failure."

Hannah laughed. "All right."

"I'll be home before supper, and if you or your mother need me before then, just send Junior to the Mills family. He'll find me there."

CHAPTER TWENTY-TWO

One thing that Caroline had always loved about Hannah, ever since they met, was the way the other woman just went ahead and did what she thought best, without asking for permission or approval. She'd been that way from the very beginning—even their first night on the Oregon Trail, when she'd showed Caroline how to cook over a campfire despite the latter having been completely in over her head. And she had done it again now, insisting that Caroline get out of her doldrums and talk to her about what was going on in her mind.

Not only had their conversation helped remind Caroline that she was not alone, but it had also sparked the beginning of an idea—the first step of a brave, desperate chance she might have to change things.

Plus, of course, Caroline could take inspiration from Hannah and do what she thought was best before asking for permission to do so.

After leaving the Sullivan camp midmorning on an overcast day in November, Caroline crossed through the camp to where the Millses had made their temporary home on the far edge. Though she didn't really expect to see Daniel anywhere nearby, she was nevertheless disappointed not to find him there. He had returned from a long day of traveling the night before, and already he had a full day again. As she approached, Caroline noticed both of the Mills women, mother and daughter, chopping vegetables near their wagons; she said a silent prayer that Abby would notice her first. She cleared her throat, trying to step more heavily as they got closer, as though warning a wild animal that she was present so as not to startle them.

"Caroline!" Abby said with evident delight. "We weren't expecting you."

Mrs. Mills smiled stiffly and turned her focus back to her task, allowing her daughter to play hostess for once.

"Daniel is helping lay stones for the blacksmith, I think," Abby continued, coming to meet Caroline.

"Oh, I assumed something like that. I actually came to see you."

Abby's expression became one of polite surprise. "That's . . . wonderful! What can I do for you?"

Caroline looked over her shoulder at Mrs. Mills before turning back to Abby. "Let's take a walk."

Abby nodded in understanding. Caroline gestured toward the trail leading toward the river into town, and the two girls made their way out of the camp.

As they made small talk about the weather and about the latest supply of dry goods Daniel had brought back from the fort, Caroline surreptitiously directed their steps to the same copse of trees where she had previously left Abby with Junior Sullivan and their secrets.

"What are we doing here?" Abby looked around hopefully.

"Well, I wanted to find somewhere that we could talk—hopefully without being heard."

Abby stopped looking for Junior and gave all her attention to Caroline. "What are we doing here?" she asked again, more warily.

"You're going to help me."

Abby blinked at her in surprise but didn't try to hide her mischievous smile. "Ooh . . . all right, what am I helping you with?"

"You're going to help me get your mother to like me."

Abby burst out laughing. "What makes you think I can do that? Have you noticed that she doesn't seem too happy with me either?"

"Of course she does. She's your mother."

"Caroline." The tone of Abby's voice made her feel as though she had missed something important, as though she were a child who had no business engaging with the grown-ups. "My mother worships the ground Daniel walks on and no one else even comes close. Sure, she loves me because I'm her daughter, but I'm not convinced she likes me all that much."

"That can't be true!"

Abby shrugged matter-of-factly. "Ask Daniel. He won't admit it completely, but there are always times when he needs to step in and defend me against her criticism."

Caroline didn't have more than a handful of memories of her own mother, but she could just as easily compare Abby's mother to Mrs. Sullivan. Even when under the stress of losing her husband and one of her children over the last six months, Mrs. Sullivan had been the image of grace and understanding. She never raised her voice; she never spoke a harsh word. There had been times that she had withdrawn into herself, quietly managing what must have been a mountain of pain, but she had never once made any of her children feel as though they weren't loved and cherished.

Mrs. Mills, on the other hand, had already shown herself to be capable of the very biting criticism that Abby mentioned, without any of the same stress.

"I'm sorry," Caroline said. "I'm sure you're right. It must be hard having a mother like that, but . . ." She felt tears of frustration welling up. "I just don't know what else to do. I talked to Hannah about it this morning, and . . . You must have *some* idea, some suggestion, don't you? Some way to at least keep the peace with your mother?"

"Are you sure you want to marry into this family?"

Caroline stared at her in shock. "Excuse me?"

"I just mean . . . well, we're talking about the rest of your life, aren't we? And it's already not easy. Imagine what could happen in the future."

"I'm not second-guessing Daniel."

"Of course not." Abby smiled and seemed to back off from this line of questioning. "And you'll likely always have the Sullivans as your second family, won't you? That must make you feel quite fortunate."

Caroline moved to sit on a fallen tree that stretched across the grass. "I am fortunate. You're right. I'm also extremely frustrated. I feel as though I've been doing everything I know how to do to be the exact person that your mother—and brother—want me to be, and none of it is right. Of course Daniel loves me, but if things are going to continue to be strained with your mother . . . I don't know how long that will last." She looked at Abby with desperation. "Isn't there anything you can think of? Or . . . anyone you've heard your mother praise? Any hint of what it might take to at least get in her good graces?"

Abby looked thoughtful and came to sit next to Caroline.

"Let me think . . . There must be someone. I haven't paid terribly close attention, you know. Once they all decided we were coming west to Oregon I figured any chance I had to make my own choices was long gone."

She leaned forward on her knees, staring into the middle distance as she pored over her memories. While Abby thought, Caroline was consumed by memories of her own. Of the first time she had noticed Daniel Mills, way back on the streets of Independence, Missouri. Of the time that he'd kept her from being bit by a snake, or the time that he'd read out loud to her from one of her favorite books.

After her entire life had been upended, Daniel had been one of the first people who had showed her what her new life could be. Between him and Hannah, Caroline had managed to find a safety and stability in the midst of the wilderness, and no matter whatever else they went through, she would always be grateful for that.

"You know," Abby began, "I love my mother. I do. And she's going to be so good for this town, as is my father. But as I sit and think about what you might be able to do to help her like you more, I'm kind of at a loss. She's stingy with her praise. The only thing that has come to mind so far—other than how much she adores Daniel—is, actually . . ." Abby laughed awkwardly. "I think she might have thought a good deal of the Hudson sisters. In her own way, of course. But did you know she asked Annie Hudson to lead a quilting circle?"

"I'd heard that, yes."

"And when we had to give a toll to the Shoshone when we crossed their land, Mama was surprisingly impressed with the luxury and quality of the big mirror the Hudsons offered. I don't know that she cares about material things, so to speak, but I do think she is so protective of her family—of Pa and Daniel, at least—that she is constantly looking for ways they might be taken advantage of. It's a constant vigilance that puts her on edge more often than not and leads her to expecting the worst of people. It's not easy to deal with, truth be told. So I suppose in a way the fact that the Hudsons were traveling west without a man and still managed to support themselves so thoroughly gave her an admiration for them. Maybe grudging, but admiration all the same. Of course, being a seamstress is one of the very few ways that a woman can earn an income without being looked down on, so I'm sure that makes a difference."

"Amy Cole said that you were making braided rugs to sell. Is that somehow tied to your mother's opinion on such things?"

Abby blushed, cleared her throat, and shook her head. "No. Um . . . no, no, that's just so I have . . . something. I like to be independent, I suppose, is all it is. I thought it might be useful to start saving money when I can, and we have more than enough fabric that I can make some in my free time. What did you do before you came west?"

"Nothing," Caroline said miserably. "I don't know how to do anything like that. You know I love your brother, but most of why I am so eager to be married to him and have a home of my own is because I don't know how else I will be able to make it out here on the frontier."

"Well, don't let Mama hear you say that," Abby said with a sympathetic grin. "She'll skip right over the 'you loving him' part and only hear the 'you can't do anything on your own' part."

"Except hunt," Caroline muttered. "The one thing I try to do on my own and she doesn't approve of that either."

"Are you going to let that stop you? The way Junior described it to me, you seemed really happy that day. Proud of yourself."

"I was. And, you know, I never thought it would be something I would ever attempt, let alone enjoy, but there's such a boon in being able to provide for myself and my family in that way. Unfeminine though it may be."

"To be honest, Caroline, that might just be a choice you have to make. It's something I realized a couple years ago, when I first started getting that itch to make things to sell to others. I started with just some small bouquets of flowers I picked from our garden. That was before I realized all our neighbors had their own gardens, of course. Mama thought it was so unladylike and inappropriate for me to be 'seeking after filthy lucre,' as she put it."

"How is that different than what Miss Hudson did?"

"Well, you understand," she said with exaggerated sarcasm, "Louisa Hudson didn't *ask* anyone to hire her. She waited for them to come to her. Not like my going door to door trying to sell my sad bouquets." She rolled her eyes. "But eventually I realized I was never going to be happy sticking to the strict guidelines that she had in mind for me. And there are far too many years ahead of me to already settle on being unhappy."

Caroline looked at her, curious and confused. "How old are you? When did you get so smart?"

"Having an older brother like Daniel helps," Abby said, nudging Caroline playfully with her shoulder.

"I'm not sure I'm quite ready to give up on at least getting on your mother's good side. I suppose I'll just have to find some other way to show her that I'm not someone she has to protect her son from."

"Good luck."

"Yes." Caroline sighed. "Thank you. Do you really not have any other secret trick you can tell me about?"

"If I did, I would tell you." After a moment of silence, Abby spoke up again hesitantly. "Can I ask for your help now?"

"Of course! I mean, I'm surprised. I thought we had just established that I'm generally useless, but . . ."

"I'm not even going to respond to that," Abby said lightly. "You are exactly who I need help from."

Caroline raised her eyebrows expectantly.

"I need to see Junior again."

"Abby—"

"Come on, Caroline. You know what it's like to have

my mother's disapproval. Imagine if she forbade Daniel from seeing you."

"Now that's not a fair comparison at all."

"Please, Caroline. I promise not to get you in trouble. I just need a little help."

Caroline looked at the younger girl, her expression hopeful and anguished. She recognized the same desperation in herself, the not having anywhere else to turn, the not knowing what she would do without the security of the man she loved.

"What do you want me to do?"

CHAPTER TWENTY-THREE

Against her better judgment, Caroline allowed Abby to talk her into becoming an ally and secret-keeper in the younger girl's courtship with Junior Sullivan. There was a whole plan involving what excuses Junior would make, and how all Caroline needed to do was keep suspicion from falling their way. She thought about admitting that she had already told Hannah, and how well she had taken it, but then felt ashamed for having already divulged the secret.

Instead, Caroline decided to just agree to whatever Abby wanted. She told herself that it wouldn't be for long—either the relationship would fizzle out or would progress enough that Abby would have to be honest with her parents. If Caroline could help the two young people stay out of trouble before that happened, she didn't see that there was much harm. Junior was an admirable young man—he wouldn't do anything that would make her regret this.

And she had to admit to herself that there was an

element of pleasure in rebelling against Mrs. Mills just this little bit, even if the older woman didn't know it. And hopefully she never would.

But at the same time, Caroline never stopped turning the problem over in her mind. Even as she kept this secret from Mrs. Mills, she was trying to find some way to show Daniel's mother that she was all the things the woman wished for her son: capable, ladylike, and whatever other seemingly contradictory assets.

It was this thorny problem that still occupied Caroline, a couple days later, when she and Hannah took up the project of completely sorting through and repacking the Sullivans' two covered wagons.

"When does Mr. Mills think your mother's house will be done?" Caroline asked as Hannah handed off a half-full wooden trunk to her.

Hannah was inside the family's supply wagon, hauling everything from within to the back, where Caroline would take it from her and spread it all out in the dirt and grass around the campsite. Once they had everything out and visible, the women could make decisions about what could be kept, what needed to be repaired, what they might need to get rid of, and what new things they should ask Ben and Daniel to buy the next time they traveled to Fort Vancouver.

"Well, remember," Hannah said, "this is secondhand, the mayor telling Junior, who then has to remember to tell Ma once he's back here. And though we both know my brother is growing up to be a fine young man, we also both know he is not always the most focused or reliable at the moment."

Caroline laughed. Only the night before, he had

wandered off to talk to Caleb, the blacksmith's apprentice, while eating supper, returning an hour later without the bowl and spoon he had left with. His mother sent him back to the Gilroys' camp immediately, with threats that he wouldn't be able to eat in the morning without it.

"But what Junior says is that the men are clearing our claim today and tomorrow. And then more of the men will be available to help with the construction at the beginning of next week."

"So . . . possibly by the end of the month?"

"By the end of the month," Hannah repeated with a grin. "Maybe before. Ben claims that our house will be ready soon, too, but as we've already discussed, I'm not going to get my hopes up. That would make me far too likely to jump into a new project like, oh, I don't know, trying to build a bed frame well before we're ready, and then I would have to find somewhere to store it and figure out how to move it and then get frustrated with myself. You know how I can be."

Hannah chuckled and handed down to Caroline a small, wooden side table that looked as though it belonged in a fine parlor back east.

"Goodness, I didn't even know this was back there!" Caroline said when she saw it.

"There are a few little fripperies and fineries Ma tucked away. Most of them are small and light, but this table was made by her grandfather in Norway and brought all the way across the ocean. She wasn't about to leave this behind."

Caroline carefully set the table close to the wagon, where it could stay out of the way and safe. When she turned back to Hannah, the latter already had another big trunk perched halfway over the side.

"This one's yours," she said. "And it's pretty heavy. Do you want to hold it there, and I'll come down and help?"

Caroline tested the weight and nodded. Her whole life, it seemed, had been relegated to this single trunk. When her brother had dragged her away from New York City, she'd had time to grab a few belongings, only to quickly learn that most of those things were utterly useless on the Oregon Trail. When her wagon finally broke an axle and she'd had to shed more of her things, everything worth keeping for the most part fit in this trunk.

Hannah carefully took the other side of the trunk, and the two women pulled it down out of the wagon, little by little, as the weight shifted.

"Just a reminder," Caroline said, straining a little under the heavy wooden piece, "that a year ago I would have fainted at a dance if my stays were too tight."

Hannah laughed, gasping for breath. "Don't! You'll make me drop it!"

With an awkward sideways shuffle away from the wagon, they reached a clear spot of ground to set down the trunk.

"Phew!" Hannah said, wiping sweat from her brow with her sleeve as she straightened again. "I had forgotten how much you had in there."

"Everything I have to my name."

Caroline knelt in the dirt in front of her trunk and carefully undid the latch. Hannah had already disappeared into the wagon again, perhaps to give her some privacy. With her only two dresses rotating between being worn and being washed, Caroline hadn't really had a reason to go into this trunk for weeks since she'd last packed it away.

Her first impression upon raising the lid was a slight whiff of whiskey that reminded her of her brother, John. That had always been a part of his business meetings and the suppers that he'd hosted at their townhouse in New York City. Though the drinking had escalated as the Oregon Trail grew more difficult, to Caroline it still offered the memory of those nights in the city when she had felt so proud of her enterprising brother, so cared for as he managed their family business.

The top level of the trunk was a simple, folded gray shawl—far too light to be of use in these Pacific Northwest winters, but maybe she could bring it out again in the spring. Caroline lifted it out and set it in her lap to keep it out of the dirt. Just underneath was a collection of smaller items: several books, her brother's gloves, an extra box of ammunition, a handheld mirror, a hammer she'd never seen him use, and a small ceramic thimble.

Caroline touched each of them in wonder, remembering when she had gotten each.

"Oh, good, yes, take a break," Hannah called breathlessly as she heaved another heavy-looking barrel out of the wagon. "Don't mind me."

"I'll be right there," Caroline called back with a grin.

When she turned back to the trunk, the first thing her eyes lit on was the small piece of lace she'd used to wrap up her pearl necklace when she had finally taken it off. With a tiny gasp, she picked it up, opened it, and gazed on the most valuable thing she had ever owned in her life—likely the most valuable thing she ever would own.

Not long before she'd had to leave New York City, her then-beau Phillip Ross had given her this exquisite, delicate pearl necklace. She had worn it proudly as evidence of his devotion. When her brother had made her travel west, Caroline had clung to the meaning imbued in that piece of jewelry. Day after day, she'd told herself he loved her, that the necklace meant he wanted her to be his wife—but she'd been disappointed again and again, until it finally became clear that Phillip was not coming after her. So she had tucked the necklace away. Though his inconstancy had hurt her, she'd at least had the presence of mind to be grateful enough for this gift to not let it go to waste.

Abby's words about needing to show she wasn't someone Daniel needed to be protected from echoed in her mind. The luxury of the Hudsons' mirror had impressed her; maybe this could too.

Maybe Daniel's mother would never be impressed that Caroline had managed to bag a rabbit her first time hunting. Maybe she would never truly appreciate the lengths to which Caroline had gone to become as competent as she now was, the trials and errors she had suffered even while struggling for survival on the trail. But it seemed likely that even June Mills would not turn her nose up at the amount of cash a necklace like this could be worth. This kind of windfall could secure Daniel and Caroline for years.

She realized, of course, that the wild frontier of the territories made for a very unstable market, but given what Daniel had told her about Fort Vancouver, it didn't seem impossible that she might find a buyer there.

It was something. And it was a better plan than she or Hannah or Abby had managed to come up with so far. Maybe this way of gaining funds was more ladylike—in Mrs. Mills's eyes—than what she had shamed her daughter for. And certainly more than hunting.

Caroline fastened the strand around her neck for safety, closed the trunk, and stood.

"I have an idea! I'll be right back," she called to Hannah, who was digging through what seemed to be a sack of old clothes.

"You keep doing this!" Hannah protested, half-laughing. "When are you going to tell me about all these ideas of yours?"

"When one of them works. When is Ben going to Fort Vancouver next?"

"Soon. Tomorrow or the day after, I think."

"Do you know where he is today?"

Hannah shook her head. "There are so many buildings going up . . . I think he was just going where he's needed."

Caroline nodded, setting her jaw. "Do you think you could do all this"—she gestured to the family's belongings strewn across the dirt—"on your own for a bit? I need to find him."

"Of course. Is everything okay?"

"Maybe. Hopefully. I think so."

CHAPTER TWENTY-FOUR

Fortunately, Caroline was able to track Ben down relatively quickly. As she walked down the widening trail from the campsite to where the center of Eden Valley would be when the town was completed, she scanned the horizon, looking for signs of progress. With the tall trees and rolling hills in all directions, there was only so far that she was able to see, only so many of the construction sites that were visible from this vantage.

One of the closest land claims to the center of town was that of the Martells—the doctor wanted to be near everyone as possible, and the new mayor had arranged a general agreement from all the other men to allow that. Their small, one-room-for-now cabin was going up quite nicely now, and from this distance Caroline could see a group of men bustling around, getting the walls up. Though she could clearly see the work being done, it was still a decent walk away, through a stretch of landscape that had only barely begun to see trails forming.

As Caroline picked her way through the tall grass,

she thought about what the money from selling this pearl necklace could mean for her and Daniel. She had a vague idea that the Mills family was rather well-off—they had herded almost two dozen cattle all the way west, after all, and Mr. Mills had always held sway among the community. She had never questioned Daniel's ability to provide for her. But even so, the absolute privilege and luxury of having cash on hand was potentially life-changing.

At the same time, she harbored a deep fear—so deep that she succeeded in stuffing it down, hopefully to be forgotten—that Daniel would resent her for asserting herself in this way. That he would somehow agree with his mother's opinion that she was unladylike or acting inappropriately. But calling up the memory of his expression when he had seen her learning to shoot banished that fear. He had taught her to wield a rifle; he wanted her to be able to stay safe. No, she was afraid for no reason. Daniel would support her being able to take care of herself.

Caroline picked her way across the narrow trail toward the Martells' homestead, remembering the way her betrothed had smiled at her as he taught her to set the rifle's stock against her shoulder.

Daniel Mills loved her. He admired her strength and how she had gotten through everything since leaving New York. Selling her pearl necklace that she would never wear, in exchange for actual greenbacks or gold they could use to help fund their life, would be a choice that he supported.

She knew that. Or, at least, she vowed to remind herself often enough that it would feel more certain.

Caroline lifted her chin and approached the group of men all working together to build Dr. Martell's home. She wouldn't let any doubt show on her face. She would get this done as best she could and take the steps to help her settle better into the Mills family.

"Ben! Benjamin Findley!"

Half a dozen men were clustered around felled logs; it looked as though they were stripping the trees of their bark. One of the shorter men disconnected from the mass, removed his hat, and squinted at her. "Miss Harper?" He crossed the dirt clearing to her.

"Oh, you know you can call me Caroline," she returned with a friendly smile. "Listen, can we talk about something, um . . . something private?"

"Of course."

He led her closer to the small cluster of pine trees that would stand at the edge of the Martells' property. The land here was so green and so lush; even though Caroline didn't know a thing about farming or gardening, she had a suspicion she'd be able to figure it out without issue.

"What can I help you with?" Ben asked as he turned toward her. "Is everything all right with Hannah?"

"Oh! Yes, goodness, I'm sorry—I didn't even think that your mind might go there. No, this is actually something I wanted to ask you for . . ." She cleared her throat and stood taller. "For me. And if we could keep this between us, I would very much appreciate it. I would rather no one else know what I'm about to ask you."

The man looked wary, surely reluctant to take on anyone else's business or secrets. "But Daniel knows, doesn't he?"

"No, no. Not yet. I'd like to keep this from Daniel most of all. At least at first. It's . . . I promise, it's nothing scandalous or hurtful. And, believe me, if I could take care of it on my own, I wouldn't be bothering you. But . . . I need help, Ben. And I don't have anyone else I can turn to." Her voice wavered at the end, despite her best efforts. She didn't want him thinking she was too emotional or hysterical to make this decision.

He frowned his concern. "All right, all right. I'll do what I can."

"Thank you. I'm hoping it won't be that strenuous. Hannah told me you would be going to Fort Vancouver in the next day or two—is that still true?"

He nodded. "Daniel and I were hoping to take a longer, more substantial trip, maybe buy a couple wagons to fill and bring back, but the doc says he's going to need more alcohol for sterilization before we can do that. It'll just be a turnaround trip. Only as much as my horse can carry. I hope you don't need anything too hefty?"

"No—actually the opposite." Caroline touched the pearls that sat against her throat. "Do you think the fort would be a place that you could sell this necklace?" She indicated the strand resting on her collarbone.

It was clear that Ben had given literally no thought to Caroline's attire until she had actually said the word "necklace." His eyes just about fell out of his head when he saw the strand around her neck. Even a person inexperienced with fine jewelry could see this was a piece with value.

Caroline waited, holding her breath, for his answer.

Ben took a small step toward her, peering more carefully at the pearls. He nodded, chewing his lip as he thought. "I think so. It's a big, busy place, and there are all kinds of folks that come through there. You know it's right on the border, right? French. British. All kinds of men in and out. And winter is about starting, so a lot of the trappers are getting all their supplies and things." He nodded again, more certain. "Yes, I think maybe I can do something with that. I can't promise anything though."

Caroline unclasped the pearls and set them carefully in Ben's open palm. "This is more valuable than anything else I own. I'm trusting you with this."

"What do you need the money for?"

"Nothing, really. Or, rather, nothing specifically. It's more that . . . well, it was a gift from an old beau, so I don't really need to keep it, but also I thought, as Daniel and I get closer to being able to build our home and start our family . . ." She blushed, afraid she had been too personal. "It's just another way that I can help out with everything."

"But you don't want him to know?"

"I just want to be able to surprise him. At the right time. I don't want to burden him with one more responsibility, and I'm hoping it will fetch a good amount of money. One that feels like a celebration of sorts. I just want everything to be perfect."

"All right, then," Ben said, coiling the necklace carefully and placing it in the front pocket of his shirt. He wore a hesitant grin. "I'll do what I can."

"Thank you," Caroline gushed. "Oh, thank you so much. I trust you to get the best price you can. Mostly I'm just eager to have this memory behind me, you know? The man who gave me that . . . well, I'll never see him again. Might as well never see the necklace again and get some savings in the bargain."

"Course." He looked back over his shoulder to where the men still worked over the logs. "I should get back to it, if that's all you needed."

"It is, yes." Caroline hesitated, struck all of a sudden by the fact that she'd just handed over a valuable pearl necklace, never to be seen again, putting all her hopes in this one man who truthfully she didn't know all that well.

But Daniel knew him. Hannah knew him and loved him. Caroline herself would have plenty of time to get to know Benjamin Findley. There was nothing for her to worry about.

She followed him back to where close to two dozen men darted here and there, tools in hand, some yelling instructions, some just putting their heads down to work. For not the first time, Caroline reflected that it was lucky she and her brother had joined such a large company to come west on the Oregon Trail. They might have been slower to travel at times, less efficient in the need to keep everyone together, but now, as they all pitched in to help one another before any snow fell, the larger community was a boon. So many hands spread all the work around.

She watched only a few minutes, but in that time she didn't see any sign of Junior Sullivan. Caroline tried to remember if he had told his family where he would be spending the day that morning, but the overwhelming project of helping Hannah repack the wagons dominated her memory.

As she waved goodbye to Ben and began her walk back to the camp, Caroline resolved not to worry about it. Junior was a grown man—or close enough to it—and there was nothing to be concerned about. There were plenty of other places in the burgeoning town where he could be lending a hand, and Abby surely would have told her if there was some secret place he was sneaking off to.

Even as she told herself this explanation, Caroline wondered if she should check in on Abby. As almost the only person who knew that couple's secret, she felt a sense of responsibility for them.

But by the time she made it back to the Sullivans' camp, all thoughts of meddling had left her mind. Caroline returned to find Hannah sitting in the bare dirt, her head hanging down between her knees and the detritus and projects of their life scattered around her.

"Hannah Sullivan," she exclaimed as she hurried up. "You didn't unpack all this without me, did you?"

Hannah looked up at her, squinting at the midday sun. "Oh, good. You're back. We gotta get all this packed back in."

Shaking her head at her friend's seemingly endless energy, Caroline helped Hannah to her feet.

CHAPTER TWENTY-FIVE

The next day, Benjamin Findley traveled north to Fort Vancouver and returned without any fanfare or even careful attention from anyone else in town. Caroline worried and fretted about his safety—there were miles and miles of wilderness, animals, and even Indians between Eden Valley and Fort Vancouver. If anything happened to her necklace there would be nothing she could do, and Caroline would have lost the only real thing of value she owned.

"Do you think he'll come by to see you when he gets back?" she asked Hannah, for what must have been the fourth time.

They had finished repacking the family's supply wagon the night before and had spent this day airing out their sleeping wagon. The cots, blankets, pillows, and every other piece of comfort that had lived under that canvas for months needed to be cleaned. Caroline had just returned from gathering a large basketful of tall grass that they would hopefully be able to dry out before it rained again. Once dry, they would then use it to fill the mattresses with fresh stuffing. As she lay out the handfuls of grass across the wagon at regular intervals, Caroline tried to put her worries about Ben and her necklace out of her mind.

"Well, he always has before, but he also knows I understand if he doesn't. Which is the same thing I told you earlier." She peered at Caroline, brow furrowed. "Now, I recognize that there is likely something that you are not ready to tell me, but if you are not going to talk about it, I would ask that you at least stop talking around it so much. You're worrying me."

"I know, I know." Caroline threw up her hands in frustration at herself. "As soon as I talk to him, I promise I'll tell you. I just can't—"

"Hello, ladies."

Both Caroline and Hannah turned at the sound of the voice. It was Ben, approaching with arms open for a hug from his fiancée. Hannah ran to meet him, while Caroline relaxed in relief that he had at least returned in one piece. She let out a long, slow breath as the two embraced, then proceeded to bite her tongue in order to keep herself from interrupting out of her desperation for news.

"How was it?" Hannah asked, taking his hand and leading Ben to sit by the campfire, Caroline hesitantly following.

"Crowded. Beaver-trapping season is starting. I ate a hot meal at a tavern just outside the walls of the fort and listened in on a conversation with some of the old-timers. Apparently more and more trappers coming out west every year has netted each one fewer and fewer pelts. You should have seen their expressions at seeing all the new blood walking around stocking up on jerky and what-not for the winter. They were noticeably warmer toward me when they learned I was settling a farm a few miles away instead of encroaching on their trapping territory."

"Were you able to get everything you went for?" Hannah asked.

Ben shifted his gaze to Caroline and nodded. "I did, yes. All of it."

Caroline felt herself relax. "It's all right, Ben. I was going to tell Hannah about it all anyway. Once I was sure."

He grinned. "In that case . . ." He reached into his front shirt pocket, where he had stashed the necklace originally, and from which he now withdrew a small leather pouch no bigger than Caroline's palm. As he handed it over to her, he explained, "Lucky break, really. One of the fur moguls was out from Boston. Seems he's been trying to convince his fiancée that the west isn't all chaos and heathens, so he bought your pearls to give to her as a sign that civilization was well on its way."

Caroline smiled at that as she peered into the pouch. "You got a good price, then?"

"I think so. To be honest, I might have trouble spending that much money if it were me. That should be a great start for you all."

Hannah was looking from one to the other with a puzzled expression on her face.

"Ben took my pearl necklace to sell for me," Caroline explained. "I thought, maybe if Mrs. Mills learned that I have this, that I can take care of myself, she might not be so protective of Daniel."

"Is *that* why?" Ben asked. "If you had told me I might have tried to talk you out of it." He chuckled.

"What?"

"I've been friends with Daniel Mills since we were about six years old. I have never wronged him or even disappointed him, and Mrs. Mills still seems a mite wary of me. There might be a way you can convince her you are worthy of her precious boy"—he grinned at this—"but you'll save yourself a lot of grief not even trying."

Caroline wilted. "Really?"

Ben grimaced. "Sorry. But, you know, if Daniel loves you—and take it from me, he does—he's not going to let his mother talk him out of it."

He turned back to Hannah as she peppered Ben with more questions about his visit to the fort, about the people he met and his adventure selling the necklace. Caroline left them alone to count over her money and think about what he had said. Was it true that what had been a big gesture for Caroline wouldn't matter to Mrs. Mills in the slightest? The Findleys had known Daniel's family for almost two decades; surely Ben would know better than anyone else how they all interacted with and influenced one another. If he said she shouldn't worry about it, she probably shouldn't worry about it.

Caroline climbed into the supply wagon and scanned the interior for her trunk.

But on the other hand, she thought, Daniel had seemed so concerned about his mother being unhappy with her.

She opened the trunk, moved aside the shawl, and

tucked her pouch of money down into the deep recesses against the right side, where she would hopefully be able to find it again easily. Just before she closed the trunk again, Caroline had second thoughts. She fished out the pouch and withdrew a single five-dollar gold Beaver coin. If she still wore gloves every day, as she had in New York parlors, she thought she might keep it in there. Instead, Caroline tucked the coin into the pocket of her apron. The weight of the coin made the garment hang a bit uneven, but she was too afraid of not having access to it if she might need it.

Next she found the Sullivans' sewing kit—her own had been woefully inadequate, and had been absorbed by Mrs. Sullivan when Caroline had started living with them. She would have to remind Daniel to obtain the supplies she needed from Fort Vancouver when they were married. With just a couple quick stitches, Caroline secured her apron pocket closed, hopefully keeping the Beaver coin safely ensconced. She couldn't have said what she thought she would need to spend that money on, but knowing she had just a small bit of resources on hand helped her feel more prepared.

Especially as it seemed she was seeing Daniel less and less.

The independence she had discovered over the two thousand miles she'd traveled from Missouri was dear to her. Even with everything feeling unanchored and uncertain, Caroline could hold on to that.

When she emerged again from the wagon, Caroline noticed that not only were Ben and Hannah even more exuberant than they had been just a few minutes before, but her mother and sisters were now gathered around as well.

"Is everything okay?" Caroline asked as she approached.

Hannah turned to her with a beaming smile. "Ben says our home will be finished in about ten days, and then we can get married!"

"Oh! That's—" Caroline beamed widely for her dear friend, pushing down her own disappointment. "Hannah, I'm so, *so* happy for you. You must let me know how I can help."

"Packing the wagon with me already helped. That will make it so much easier for me to move my few things when the time comes."

Caroline quelled her envy as she looked at the happy couple grinning at each other, reminding herself that she would have the very same, very soon.

"Of course, of course," she said. "I'm here for whatever you need."

But she wasn't sure her friend had heard her, so wrapped up was Hannah in her betrothed, surrounded by her mother and younger sisters, all of whom had questions for her. Caroline hung back, letting the Sullivan family have their moment of celebration. She would have plenty of time to spend with her friend. There were only about ten days left to get everything ready.

CHAPTER TWENTY-SIX

With the money for her pearl necklace stowed safely away in her trunk, and preparations for Hannah and Ben's wedding underway, Caroline settled in to focus on the tasks ahead of her. Keeping herself busy was exactly what she needed to help forget about her worries over Daniel, his mother, Abby, her own future, and all the uncertainties that seemed to be constantly swirling in her mind. There was so much on her mind, but Hannah's house—Hannah's wedding—were solid, reliable things that Caroline could count on. She focused all her attention on that.

The night Ben returned from Fort Vancouver with news of their homestead, Hannah had been essentially useless, so consumed was she with plans for the next chapter in her life. It wasn't often that Hannah was distracted and Caroline was steady, but she took the opportunity to repay in some small part all that her friend had done for her over the previous months. Though it took her until an hour after sunset, Caroline finished stuffing the mattresses with the newly dried grass, returning all the cleaned and aired linens to the sleeping wagon, all while making the family supper as well as cleaning up after it.

Hannah wasn't the only one distracted; her mother had burst into tears when she heard the news and couldn't think about anything else the rest of the night. This was perhaps the first time Caroline had ever seen Mrs. Sullivan completely ignoring her chores, not even excepting the days when her small son and her husband had died. But Caroline was proud to step into the gap and take care of the Sullivans the way they had always taken care of her.

Eventually, with everything finished and put away, Caroline made her excuses and went to bed when the littlest Sullivan girls did. She fell into bed that night exhausted but with the flush of accomplishment bringing her the most complete peace she had felt in a long time.

"Caroline!"

Early the next morning, Caroline was woken by Hannah shaking her gently. She opened her eyes slowly, the sun already cutting through the opening in the canvas at the back of the wagon.

"What time is it?"

"Breakfast is about ready—I didn't think you would want to miss it."

"Thank you." Caroline sat up in her cot and stretched. Her back was a bit sore from all the lifting and carrying she had been doing over the previous days, but the full night of sleep had helped a lot. Her braid had come mostly undone in the night, so as Caroline woke she began to comb out her long, wavy hair with her fingers. "How was your night? You and Ben were still chattering away when I finally went to bed."

Hannah's eyes and smile grew big as she sat back on the cot across from Caroline. She seemed as though she was so full up with what she wanted to tell her friend that she could burst.

"Once everyone went to bed and we were alone, he had *another* surprise for me. And actually, I need your help with it."

"Of course. What is it?"

"He brought back enough yards of silk to make a new dress!"

Caroline's mouth fell open. "Silk? Hannah Sullivan. Are you going to wear a *silk* wedding dress?"

She nodded excitedly. "It's this beautiful pale blue, just the color of a summer sky. Like when we fell in love. That's what he said when he gave it to me," she confided.

"Oh, goodness. I'm so happy for you. That sounds perfect! I'm not much of a seamstress though. It's too bad Louisa Hudson isn't here. You could have had the most perfect fit."

"True. But between Ma and me, we'll put together something good enough. But I need you to be the model for it."

"Me?"

Hannah nodded. "Just at first. We're practically the same size. And it will only be in the first initial fittings. But I want this dress to be unique. It will take time, and I don't know if I trust anyone else to be available when I need them to be."

"Well, of course, if you think I can help, I'm happy to. I'm just surprised."

"Come eat." Hannah stood, her neck bent a little to keep from hitting the canvas above. "And then we'll get started."

Caroline barely tasted the eggs and potatoes Mrs. Sullivan had made for breakfast; she was too consumed listening to Hannah sketch out all her plans. Now that she actually had a tentative wedding date, Hannah was clearly eager to dive into all of the things she had superstitiously put off.

"And I will need to make a list of all the things for Ben to buy at the fort for our house, and prioritize them, as well as a prioritized list of the furniture we can build. I thought we could see if we could maybe hire one of the men to help with that. If not . . . well, maybe we'll just have to put our home together little by little."

Caroline nodded along as she ate swiftly. "And whatever you need me to do among all of that I am happy to," she said after swallowing down the last of her coffee. To herself, Caroline felt grateful to have all of this to occupy her. It was a far more productive way to spend her time than her futile efforts to plead Mrs. Mills's favor.

"But first, the *dress*," Hannah said. "While you were sleeping, I pulled out the sewing kit from the supply wagon and ran across to the Hudsons' to borrow some of Louisa's straight pins."

"You're absolutely sure you want to fit it to me?" Caroline asked again.

Hannah smiled indulgently. "Better that than asking you to do any of the sewing for it," she teased.

Caroline laughed, finished the last bites of her fried potatoes, and stood. "All right. Tell me what you want me to do."

Hannah and Caroline got to work. In the privacy of the wagon, Caroline stripped down to her underthings and held out her arms, waiting for the delicate fabric to be wrapped as needed.

And continued waiting. Hannah stayed where she was, watching.

Finally she looked at Hannah. "What is it?"

Her friend grimaced. "Well . . . I can't get a true fit if you're hunched over like that. The wagon cover isn't high enough."

"What are you saying?"

Hannah began to giggle. "We have to do this outside. I'm sorry, I'm so sorry."

Caroline looked down at her petticoat and undershirt: faded, worn, in need of a wash, and in no way ever intended for public viewing. "You must be joking!"

Hannah offered her an exaggerated pout. "Please? We'll be careful. We'll wrap you in silk here and then just . . . I don't know, rewrap you when you can stand up straight?"

"How is *that* going to work?"

"I don't know. But what other choice do we have?"

"I . . ." Caroline looked around, trying to come up with some alternative other than her standing in the middle of the campsite with her petticoat clearly visible to anyone who walked by. "You know if June Mills sees me like this, any chance I have of her approval will disappear."

"She won't. I'll block you from view. It will be fine. *Please*, Caroline?"

Though her friend was trying to joke and make the entire situation seem less serious than it was, Caroline could hear the pleading in Hannah's tone. This was important to her. This was her only wedding dress, her best chance to make that day exactly what she wanted it to be.

Caroline closed her eyes, took a deep breath, and finally said, "All right. Let's just hurry."

Hannah nodded, beaming, and began to carefully drape Caroline's form with the soft fabric. "I'll do the shirtwaist part in here, so you can easily climb out of the wagon, and then we'll do the skirt part when we get down."

Caroline groaned. "I'm never going to let you forget this, Hannah Sullivan."

"Soon to be Mrs. Benjamin Findley, you mean."

In spite of Caroline's dread and embarrassment, the mood was light. To her, the whole situation was so silly, so unexpected, there wasn't anything else she could do but go along with her friend's instructions and laugh. After tucking the rolled-up silk under her arm, she scrambled down out of the wagon with Hannah close behind her. Hurrying and holding their breaths, the two women did their best to quickly situate the blue fabric around Caroline in a way that at least approximated a dress before anyone else walked by the campsite to see her level of undress. All the while, a voice in the back of her mind whispered, *Unladylike!* again and again, though she quelled it as best she could.

"Measure twice, cut once," Mrs. Sullivan said. She

and the younger Sullivan girls had been practicing reading out loud while Caroline and Hannah worked, trying to stay out of their way.

"Oh, I intend to measure half a dozen times," Hannah returned. "Without a pattern, I need to be more than sure."

"Yes, explain to me how you're doing this without a pattern?" Caroline asked.

"The only pattern we brought west is for the kind of everyday dress that silk is no good for. I've made that dress at least a dozen times. I know the build well enough that I think I can make my own with the necessary alterations."

"That's remarkable. Have you ever done that before?"

"Once. That turned out better than expected, but it wasn't a fabric like this. That's what all these pins are for—to mark the edges of where the pattern would tell me to cut. This could be an absolute failure."

"I believe in you."

Hannah continued to adjust the fabric, pulling out bits here where a flounce would go, tightening bits around the waist. Every so often she would take a few steps back to look at the silhouette and full effect of the dress. Caroline felt like a doll mixed with a pincushion, holding still for her friend, who instructed that she lift her arms periodically to check the fit.

The whole process took longer than Caroline expected—but then, she hadn't realized she would be actually helping Hannah create the pattern itself.

They ate a stand-up lunch, munching on cold biscuits left over from supper the night before. Mrs. Sullivan lamented that they wouldn't take the time to eat any of the bacon she had made, but neither Caroline nor Hannah wanted to risk getting any grease or other unsightly stain on the precious blue silk. As they worked, Caroline entertained Hannah with stories of her dressmaker in New York, the gossip she would hear when she went for fittings, the almost-fights that would break out when a customer discovered that a specific lace trim was out of stock. All in all, it was a surprisingly refreshing way to spend the morning.

"All right," Hannah said, after they had been at it for hours. "I think I know what I'm doing now."

"You're sure?" Caroline asked.

She nodded resolutely. "Yes. Let me just make a couple tiny marks with the pencil, and then you can change."

Caroline held as still as she could while Hannah very carefully deconstructed the gown she had spent hours putting together. She had to periodically pause to redo something—refold a pleat or straighten the line of a pin again—but eventually she set Caroline free.

After she had again donned her own dress, Caroline emerged from the wagon to see how else she could help Hannah. Her friend sat on an overturned bucket, the silk spread across her lap, as she carefully inspected where she had put all the pins.

"Caro!"

Caroline turned, her heart uplifted at the familiar voice.

"Daniel?"

He was closer than she had expected, and it was lucky she had just finished getting dressed again. She watched Daniel striding purposefully across the dirt toward the Sullivans' camp, his arms outstretched.

Without a thought, without any of the doubts that had plagued her over the last few days, Caroline stepped easily and eagerly into his waiting hug. "I wasn't sure when I would see you," she said, her face pressed into his shoulder.

"I know. I'm sorry. I've been—"

"Busy," she finished for him, lightly. "I know. I understand. It's just a lot. What are you doing here now?"

"It is a lot," he agreed. "But I got away a bit early, specifically so I could see you. What are you doing the rest of the day?"

She blinked at him in confusion. "I . . . um, I have no idea. Whatever Hannah needs from me, I guess."

"Hannah, can I steal her away?" he called over Caroline's shoulder.

"For now. Bring her back to me safely," Hannah called back. "We have a wedding to plan!"

"Where are we going?" Caroline asked.

"You'll see." Daniel took her hand and led her through the camp.

CHAPTER TWENTY-SEVEN

After following him only a few yards, Caroline realized that Daniel was taking her to his own campsite. She sent up a silent prayer that his mother would not be present, that nothing would mar this heaven-sent chance to spend the afternoon with him.

"How did you get away early?" she asked him as they walked hand in hand between the other wagons. "I'm of course not complaining. I'm just surprised. I would think the men would be working until sunset every day."

"A lot are. But as more of the houses get completed, the labor is not stretched quite so thin. More men are getting to take breaks of an afternoon instead of each of us working ourselves to the bone."

"That's good, right?"

"Well, it's not ideal, especially as the days get shorter, but we all need a little bit of energy still to finish up the structures. Men are getting injured more as their energy and attention flag. Pa seems to think it will all work out, and I won't argue with him."

"Especially if that means you get to see me," Caroline offered teasingly.

"Precisely. I had intended to use my afternoon to go hunting," he said as they reached his family's camp. "And then I thought maybe you would want to go with me."

Daniel walked on ahead of her toward one of his wagons. None of the rest of the Mills family was anywhere in sight, but Caroline felt blindsided. Unsure and hesitant. She thought she had misheard him, but he climbed into the wagon before she could ask him to repeat himself. She tentatively closed the distance until she was waiting outside of the wagon for him.

When Daniel emerged again, he carried a rifle in each hand and wore a leather satchel hanging across his back.

"Hunting," Caroline said. "You want *me* . . . to go *hunting*."

She was too stunned to even articulate all the reasons she was confused, but deep inside hope bloomed.

"This is the gun that you learned on," Daniel said, holding out one of the rifles to her. "I know you have your brother's, but since this one is lighter it might be easier for you."

"Hunting," she said again. "What about everything your mother said about me—about how inappropriate it was? I don't . . . Daniel, I cannot give her any more reasons to disapprove of me. You have to understand how important this is to me."

Daniel smiled, abashed. "I'm not going to flaunt this in front of her, but even if she finds out somehow, surely the fact that you are doing this with me will be enough to placate her. I think so, anyway. I'll talk to her. I should have talked to her before, but everything was stressful, and I just couldn't see how much it was affecting you. I'm sorry. That was a mistake. And this is my way of making it up to you."

Caroline took the rifle from him, feeling the weight of it in her hands. "I haven't seen you much. How did you know how it was affecting me?"

"Something Ben said. It was barely a mention, but I realized that if he knew that you were feeling desperate enough to talk to him about it then it must be bad. You're not exactly the type to go airing your frustrations to anyone who will listen."

"What did he say?"

"I don't remember. Not much." He waved off her question. "Abby mentioned something too. I'm so sorry, Caro. I know this has all been hard. But I'll do better. We'll get through this together."

"All right." She nodded. "Thank you." Grinning, Caroline added, "I have been wanting to go hunting again, actually. I think I could be good at it, but I need more practice."

He stepped closer to her, so close she could feel his breath on her face. Her heart pounded and she raised her face to Daniel's as he smiled down at her.

"I'll make sure you get all the practice you need. Now," he said, his voice low, "the only thing we have to worry about is the impropriety of being alone in the woods together."

Caroline couldn't keep the smile from her face, but still she was hesitant. "You promise you'll protect me from your mother?"

"I promise."

"Then let's go see what we can get."

Holding his sister's rifle carefully, Caroline took an offered canteen and jubilantly followed him. Daniel led her past the edge of the campsite, into the woods that stretched eastward into the mountains. Caroline was happy to follow, grateful to learn anything she could from him.

The rest of their afternoon was short—Daniel wanted to be back before supper—but it was full. Learning from Daniel was different than it had been with Junior, picking up a bigger variety of tricks and tips from the different teacher. Even more than she had before, she felt as though this was a task she could be good at and bemoaned the expectations that Mrs. Mills was heaping on her.

Daniel led her deep into the woods, closer to the foothills than she had been on earlier expeditions. The forest here was so thick that at times they lost sight of the sky altogether. He pointed out the ferns, moss, and other plant life to look for that indicated a water source. They sat in silence and watched for at least thirty minutes. Caroline found herself hearing sounds—the breeze, birds in the undergrowth—that she had never noticed before.

Traveling west had been jarring enough, but now that she actually lived in a frontier town and nature was becoming more a part of her daily life, Caroline wondered if there was any part of her that was the same person she had been in New York City. She took a deep breath of the damp, the plants, the hint of animal musk, and she felt at peace.

Daniel touched her shoulder gently, and she looked

to where he pointed. Only fifteen feet away stood a deer. It looked in their direction but didn't seem to notice the two humans. Very carefully, very slowly, Daniel raised his rifle to his shoulder and took aim.

Within a couple hours, they had bagged not only the deer, but two sizable rabbits. Caroline hadn't managed to hit any of the prey herself, but Daniel was encouraging, offering her pointers and promising to take her again soon.

Daniel and Caroline finally emerged from the woods as the sun was beginning to set. Through an unspoken agreement, they had walked far enough south from where they'd started that they would not be returning to Eden Valley in any direct line of sight to the other settlers. Even though Daniel had assured Caroline more than once that his mother would not be a problem, it seemed as though neither one was willing to risk it.

And so, in the growing dusk, the pair walked back along the river down the trail, returning to the collection of covered wagons and camps from the opposite direction they had left. Daniel bore the deer over his shoulders, while Caroline carried both of the rabbits.

They had been mostly silent the several hours they had spent together, in part to better hide from their prey, but even after returning to town Caroline felt almost shy with him. It had been far too long since they had been able to spend so much time together. It had been far too long since she had been able to have an easy conversation with him, something that wasn't a fight or a negotiation. There had been a distance between them for weeks. Caroline recognized that his inviting her to hunt with him had been Daniel's attempt to bridge that gap.

It was her turn, now, to do the same.

"Thank you for making time for me," she said, looking sideways at him as they walked.

"Oh, Caro." His expression made her feel like he wanted to touch her, to take her in his arms, but didn't dare with the deer's legs hanging down over his chest. He sighed. "I always want to make time for you. I wish I had more to give you. But once we're married . . ."

"I know. So much will be different once we have our home."

"It will," he said, a fervent insistence in his tone.

And she believed him. Getting to this point had been difficult, and Caroline had had to learn to let go of what she couldn't control, but she trusted him. She knew he was doing the best with what he had.

And they would be married. Sooner or later.

"Let me walk you back to your camp," he said.

"Are you going to tell your mother that you took me hunting?"

He was silent for a moment before responding. "I'm not going to lie to her, but I likely won't volunteer the details. There are plenty of things I do every day that I don't tell her about."

Caroline nodded, though she hated the fact that Daniel felt he had to hide anything he did with her, his betrothed. But that was a fight they had already been through. That was a position with which she had already made her peace. If she wanted to be married to Daniel Mills, this was something she would likely have to get used to.

"Will I see you again before Hannah and Ben's wedding?"

"Of course. Maybe not for a whole afternoon like today, but you know I'll come see you as often as I can."

Caroline nodded again.

"I love you," she said quietly. "Thank you for spending the day with me."

"Always," he said.

CHAPTER TWENTY-EIGHT

After her afternoon with Daniel, Caroline considered going hunting again on her own. She wanted to put the new things she had learned into practice. But that was maybe the last afternoon free before Hannah got married. Her days were soon filled with all the tasks that her friend needed help with—everything from helping move pots and dishes to the new home to just listening while Hannah gushed about her plans for her spring garden.

The week before Hannah's wedding flew by. There were several more dress fittings, at least some tears when Hannah thought she had messed up the gown beyond repair, and multiple packings and repackings of Hannah's things that would be separated out from the rest of the Sullivans' when the time came.

Though she lamented not being able to afford her friend the send-off into married life she could have if they lived back east, Caroline was grateful for every step that had gotten them this far. Hannah was perfectly happy marrying without a proper trousseau. She didn't need an entire party to celebrate her engagement. This simple frontier life was exactly what she'd hoped for herself. There was nothing she wanted more than to marry her love and live in the one-room cabin he'd helped build.

This was love on the frontier. Every day Caroline was learning more and more about how good life could be even without the luxury she had grown up with. Every day she found herself grateful Ben had found a buyer for her pearl necklace that had no place in this life she was now building.

Before Caroline knew it, she was helping her friend with the final details of her wedding dress and the supper the couple would host for their family and closest friends, as well as ensuring everything she needed would be on hand as she started her married life. Even though Caroline didn't know when her own chance would come, she was happy to put everything she had into helping her dearest friend.

A few days after Daniel had taken Caroline hunting, he came by again early in the morning with a note for her.

"Abby wanted me to give this to you," he said after kissing her cheek. "I didn't read it, but she assures me you will find it very important."

Caroline unfolded the paper, glanced at the word *Junior*, and quickly folded it up again, tucking the note into the pocket of her apron. "What are your plans today?"

"Today we put the roof on Ben and Hannah's home."

"What? Really?" Hannah, hearing her own name, had

looked up from the cascade of blue silk spread over her lap.

"Really." He grinned. "So I had better get over there. The sooner the structure is finished, the sooner Ben can start moving in the couple plates and dented tea kettle he has for you all."

Hannah laughed as he waved his goodbye.

"It's more than just a couple plates," she assured Caroline. "But the tea kettle *is* dented."

Caroline laughed. "I guessed as much. What are you doing today? Are we close to finishing the dress?"

"We are!" Hannah's eyes sparkled. "I have the major cuts done and a good amount of the structure and seams sewn. There's only the details left to do—a lot of them, but that's all."

"Just tell me what you need from me. I am at your service. Today I was going to make sure all our best dresses are clean for the wedding, but anything else I can do for you I am happy to."

"What about Mrs. Mills? Did you ever figure out how you were going to get her on your side? You know I can manage without you if you need to go grovel or something."

Caroline poured a bucket of water into the pot that was placed over the campfire and then poked another handful of sticks into the fire. She knew her friend was joking—mostly. "I might be giving up on that. Daniel has assured me that he would not let that come between us, and to be honest, that just might be as good as I can hope for."

Caroline made her way to the Sullivans' supply wagon and climbed inside. She had to collect their big wash tub, as well as the soap and the washboard. Fortunately, the family had so much laundry to do all the time that the required items were easy to find.

"I'm going to go collect more water," she said once she had emerged again. "Maybe some firewood. And when I come back, you let me know what else we need to do to get you and your home ready."

With an empty bucket in each hand, Caroline made her way to the river's edge. Though she had made dozens, if not hundreds, of similar trips to creeks and springs since leaving New York City, she nonetheless still felt a kind of awe at the daily interaction with the natural world. This was part of why the idea of hunting appealed so to her, she realized. Providing for herself in such a visceral way had never been an option back east; this offered such tangible evidence of the value she could add.

Returning to the camp, Caroline promised herself that she would always recognize her own worth, even when people like June Mills tried to strip her of that. She arrived back at the Sullivans' camp surprisingly eager to wash the little girls' dresses, and whatever else she could do to make that family's life easier.

Hannah looked up at her approach. "Caroline! Did you know I'll be *married* in just a couple days?"

Caroline laughed as she set down the full buckets. "You don't say! That is brand new information."

"Thank you for doing the washing."

"Of course. You know I'm happy to do whatever I can, especially now that I've mostly figured out how to."

"What was in that note from Abby? What did she want?"

"Oh! Goodness, I completely forgot." Caroline took a couple steps away and fished the note out of her apron.

Caroline, it began, *I want you to know how much I appreciate all your help these last few weeks, and I wanted you to know that soon I don't think I'll need anything else from you. Junior and me are figuring things out, and I hope you and Daniel can too. If there's anything you want to ask of me, please do. I heard that you and Daniel went hunting a few days ago, but I haven't told Mama. Hopefully no one else will either.*

Caroline sighed, annoyed all over again at Daniel's mother and her habit of insisting upon her own way.

"It's nothing important," Caroline told Hannah. "I'm yours if you need me."

"Just the laundry, I think, for now. Later tonight, I think, Ben and I are going to go around the town to invite folks to the wedding. You're welcome to come if you want."

"That seems like the kind of thing that might be best for just the two of you, but thank you. I've got to get used to being abandoned sooner or later."

Hannah clicked her tongue in disapproval and turned her attention back to her dress; this was a mock-fight they'd already had half a dozen times.

"I think everything is going to work out nicely," Caroline continued. "Your wedding in a couple days, and then a lifetime of laundry just like this."

CHAPTER TWENTY-NINE

In what seemed like no time at all, Caroline found herself blinking back happy tears as she stood with Daniel and everyone else who loved the couple.

It was important to Hannah that she and Ben start their married life where they intended to continue it, and so she'd invited their friends to come witness their wedding in the wide-open area in front of their newly finished cabin. Caroline stood in a cluster of friends and family, her tears welling up when she saw her best friend take the hand of the man who was about to become her husband. Hannah radiated happiness. As she watched the joy on Hannah's face, Caroline felt only a fragile awe at the beauty of the love she was witnessing.

It was a cold afternoon in mid-November; the Sullivans, Findleys, Millses, and a handful of other families gathered in the thinning grass in front of the cabin that would be Ben and Hannah's home together. The sun was setting earlier and earlier, and on this particular afternoon, there would be enough time to congratulate the newlyweds before dark, but nothing more.

The final days before this monumental one had flown by. Caroline had barely had time to sit before it was the morning of the wedding and she was donning her best dress and collecting the few flowers that were still in bloom to weave into Hannah's hair.

The bride was beautiful. The groom was proud. The mothers were both teary and dispensing of all the final advice they could think of.

To Caroline, it was a touching wedding, one that she would never forget.

"I'm so happy for you, darling," she whispered to Hannah, hugging her tight after she had been made Ben's wife. "I'm devastated to lose you, but I know this is just the beginning of a wonderful new chapter for you."

"You're not losing me, Caroline Harper," Hannah scolded her gently. "You'll get your own so-called 'new chapter' soon."

"Today is about you," she said firmly. "And I already know I'm going to miss you tonight in the wagon."

Hannah responded with another fierce hug.

As she stepped back to allow the Findleys a chance to embrace the newlyweds, Caroline's gaze fell on Abby Mills. She and Junior stood close together at the edge of the crowd, talking softly to each other. Neither of them seemed to notice anyone else, so wrapped up in the other they were. Caroline wondered how long they would be able to keep the secret. She glanced at Mrs. Mills, who stood talking to the groom's mother. Well, thought Caroline, this is not my business. Abby had told her, after all, that she and Junior would likely not need her to keep their secret much longer. Whatever reveal they had planned was up to them.

The sun was sinking in the west, and the party began to break up. Mrs. Sullivan had already headed back to camp with the little girls, but Daniel was happy to walk Caroline back. There was not enough light left in the day for him to get any more work done, and Caroline was grateful for the company.

The trail from the newest Findley homestead was narrow, but straight, directing their steps to what would one day be a main road into the neighborhood. Daniel and Caroline held hands as they crossed through what would one day be a busy thoroughfare in Eden Valley.

"Well," Daniel said as they walked, "Ben and Hannah looked happy, didn't they? We'll be next, Caro."

"We will be," she repeated. "I can hardly wait. It feels so close. How is our house coming? Can I see it?"

"Soon." He grinned. "Ben has got me being superstitious like him. I don't want to get your hopes up, you know, in case something unexpected happens to keep it all from going the way I am planning. But it's started."

Caroline's smile lit up her whole face. "You didn't tell me that!"

"I told you—I don't want to let you down again, so I thought it best to not tell you right away." He grinned in return, clearly pleased to have been able to make her smile like that. "We started a few days ago. Most of the men who had finished up Ben and Hannah's home came over to help me with ours."

"Oh, Daniel." Caroline felt like skipping, she was so happy at this news. "Thank you. Just knowing that it has started means so much to me. Today, watching Hannah get everything she has wanted just reminded me that it's all possible for me too. For us. I'm so grateful."

He brought her hand to his lips and kissed it as they walked.

Caroline sighed happily, secure in his assurances that all would be settled soon.

Hannah and Ben's home was almost two miles away from the campsite where Caroline still stayed with the rest of the Sullivans and their wagons. During the long walk back, Daniel regaled her with stories about his most recent trip to Fort Vancouver for more medical supplies. It seemed the men were all more prone to injuries than they'd expected.

"Did you hear that Amy Cole has been helping Dr. Martell treat some of these injuries?"

"Yes!" she exclaimed. "She was telling us about it when Sadie and I were helping make the ballots for the mayoral vote. What kind of fourteen-year-old girl is interested in that kind of thing?"

"Oh, I don't know. Maybe the same kind of girl who will grow up to be a woman who learns how to hunt to feed her family." He winked at her.

"When I was her age I was staying home to read any chance I got."

"And what were you reading?"

Caroline paused to think, then burst out laughing. "Edgar Allan Poe. Irving's 'Legend of Sleepy Hollow.' "

"Ah," he said knowingly. "So all the dark, slightly morbid tales that a girl like Amy Cole might love reading in between helping to set a broken bone?"

"All right," she said with another laugh. "You win.

You're right. And I have to admit I like Amy, awkwardness and all. I think it's admirable how much she seems to truly not care what people might think of her. She is always only herself."

"It reminds me a bit of Abby too," he said. "I know there's a streak of rebellion in my sister, but I also think we probably wouldn't see that as much if she wasn't so confident in herself. Like Amy. And you."

Caroline thought back to the look she had seen Abby and Junior share at the wedding that afternoon.

"Speaking of your sister . . . have you noticed anything different about Abby lately?" Caroline asked.

"No . . . I don't think so. But then, you know I'm not around nearly as much as I want to be. Why? Have you?"

Caroline knew that this was the moment—if she was going to be honest with Daniel it would have to be now. But then she would be betraying Abby's trust, and Caroline didn't want to be the type of person who did that either. Hopefully she wouldn't have to keep the secret much longer.

Knowing that she would likely regret either choice, Caroline decided to trust that Abby would not get her in trouble for keeping the secret.

"Oh, I don't know. She's been very friendly and supportive with me as I've been trying to negotiate things with your mother. I'm not sure I completely understand their relationship, but it doesn't seem all that peaceful. As though Abby just keeps trying to see what she can get away with."

"It's funny you say that . . . Our grandmother had all kinds of stories about how Mama was when she was younger, always pushing the boundaries and straining beyond what was expected of her. I hadn't realized how much she had swung back the other way until she had something to say about your going off with Junior and hunting."

"Are you sure it's not just that she doesn't like Junior?" Caroline asked, thinking about Abby's reasoning for keeping their courtship secret.

"Why wouldn't she like Junior? He'll be a fine man one day."

"Why wouldn't she like *me*?" Caroline teased. "A mother's judgment isn't always logical."

"Well, in this case, I don't think her objecting to you hunting with Junior had anything to do with him. You remember what a big deal it was when Louisa Hudson insisted on going buffalo hunting."

"I suppose. Oh well. Maybe one of these days I'll learn all of your mother's rules."

"No, one of these days those rules will no longer matter. You'll be truly and irrevocably married, and then no one can criticize you."

"Wouldn't it be nice if that's the way it worked?"

Later that night, as she lay in her cot in the wagon, Caroline missed the sound of Hannah sleeping nearby, so she distracted herself by turning over her conversation with Daniel. Either he or Abby was mistaken about the way Mrs. Mills felt about Junior Sullivan, and Caroline worried that a mistake such as that could lead to a lot of heartache. Caroline just hoped that her own involvement would be minimal.

Why had she ever agreed to keep Abby's secret for her?

CHAPTER THIRTY

The morning after Hannah's wedding, Caroline woke in the Sullivans' sleeping wagon alone once again. Patience, Martha, and their mother seemed to have risen for the day already, leaving Caroline in the quiet wagon. After the adrenaline and excitement of the previous days, the chance to rest felt like a gift. Nothing specific needed to be done that day, and Caroline had been planning on giving herself a day off. Goodness knew that if her own home was close to being built, she would be busy again soon enough.

When she finally climbed out of the wagon, though, she was surprised to see that Abby Mills sat with the rest of the Sullivans as they ate breakfast.

"Did you save me any?" Caroline asked. "Good morning, Abby."

"Good morning." Abby stood and brought Caroline a cup of coffee. "I came by to see if you were free to help me today, seeing as Hannah's wedding is finally behind you."

"Help you with what?"

"Well . . . I have a couple braided rugs done, but I wanted to make a lot more. Since so many folks are getting real homes built now, maybe they need rugs and don't have time to make them, right? So I thought, since the general store will be finished soon, maybe I can see if Mr. Jameson will keep my rugs in stock. And then I won't have to go to each family myself."

All thoughts of a relaxing day of rest dissipated. Caroline couldn't say no to Daniel's sister. In fact, she realized she didn't want to. The younger girl was growing on her, and they'd built an actual friendship of sorts.

"Well, of course I'm happy to do what I can, but what does your mother think of that plan? Doesn't seem very *ladylike*," Caroline said with a wink as she sipped her coffee.

The two made their way to the seats around the campfire again. When Caroline sat, Mrs. Sullivan handed her a plate of still-hot breakfast—bacon and johnnycakes.

"Oh, you know Mama," Abby said with a shrug. "She's always got an opinion about other people's business. I figure if I get Mr. Jameson to agree first then Mama will have a harder time saying no to me."

"But you need a product to get to Mr. Jameson first," Caroline supplied.

"Precisely. Which is where you come in."

"How? I don't have any influence over him. I'd think that would be your father's wheelhouse."

"No, but if you can help me with making more, we can make it seem such an attractive and lucrative proposition that he couldn't possibly turn me down."

"And what kind of percentage in this new business venture are you offering me?"

Abby stared at her for a long moment before smiling unsurely. "Really?"

Caroline softened. "No, not really. At least, not if this is just a one-time favor to help you get things started. I can't commit to helping you with everything as long as you're doing this. I have absolutely no interest in running a business. Why do you think my brother handled everything in New York?"

"No, of course not," Abby assured her hurriedly. "But getting started is the hardest part."

"Right."

"And I thought you might want a distraction now that Hannah is gone."

"Ah . . ." Caroline smiled. "That's the real reason, isn't it?" She took another bite of the bacon, as always grateful for any meal she didn't need to cook herself.

"I don't want to overstep . . ."

"No, I'm grateful. And you're probably right, although I haven't been awake long enough to say for sure."

"Great! Then you haven't had a chance to think better of it! You're exactly who I need to help get this project started, and then if anything happens to me at least someone else knows how to continue the venture. Or end it, I suppose."

Caroline frowned at her. "Why would anything happen to you?"

"You never know. It's the wild frontier, after all." Abby stood. "Ready? We'll need to first collect any rags and discarded fabric we can get our hands on. I think a lot of the ladies are doing a fall cleaning of sorts before they move everything from their wagons to a new house. I'd like to have these ready when the store opens, and Daniel says they'll be putting the roof on it in the next week. So I thought first we would talk to the women in the bigger families, especially families with lots of boys. The Kirks, the Waterses, maybe. The kind of families that are more likely to have shirts stained beyond use or other items that they can't use anymore."

"Abby," Caroline said, putting a steadying hand on the girl's arm. "Can I eat breakfast first?"

So, instead of a relaxing day in camp resting after a busy week, Caroline had a full day of talking with other women and hauling away their discards with Abby. She was surprised to find that she very much enjoyed it. Though she had spoken true when she told Abby that she had no interest in running a business, or in regularly creating the rugs to sell to others, Caroline took a deep satisfaction in the accomplishments of that day. She was able to contribute, and by the time she climbed into bed that night she was able to rest in the knowledge that she had made a difference.

The next morning, Caroline returned to the Mills family's camp to look for Abby. They still had much to finish, and Caroline wanted to get started.

All she found was Mrs. Mills, sitting quietly by their campfire, knitting.

"Good morning," Caroline said cheerfully.

The older woman looked up at her with what seemed to Caroline to be coldness in her eyes. She gazed at Caroline flatly.

"Is, um . . . is Abby around? We were working on something yesterday, and I thought she might need more help."

Mrs. Mills set down her knitting and folded her hands in her lap. "Miss Harper, have a seat, please."

Caroline felt a current of dread run through her. Whether Mrs. Mills had sent Abby off somewhere specifically to avoid being present for this, she didn't know. Nevertheless, it seemed as though all the quiet tension and rejection from the other woman were about to see the plain light of day.

"I shouldn't stay," Caroline protested. "If Abby doesn't need me, Mrs. Sullivan is going to—"

"I won't keep you long," Mrs. Mills said with an enigmatic smile. "But there are some things I would like to say to you. A conversation we should have before you marry my son."

"All right." She sat cautiously, slowly, as though the other woman were a snake ready to strike. "What can I do for you?"

"Daniel has advised me that your house will be finished soon. I, of course, had hoped that he would have put in his effort into building a house for his father and me first, but it is clear you have bewitched him somehow."

"Excuse me?"

Mrs. Mills ignored her protest. "Young men have always made choices more with their heart than their head. I should have known my son would be no different. His father was the same way."

"He told me, actually, that when you were young you

could be impulsive, too, maybe making decisions with your heart?"

Caroline couldn't say what possessed her to challenge Mrs. Mills like that, even so benignly. Maybe she thought the older woman would be receptive to reminiscing. Or maybe she simply felt as though she had nothing else to lose. Whatever had prompted the retort, Caroline had grossly underestimated Mrs. Mills's desire to appear unimpeachably proper at all costs.

"You see, Miss Harper, this is precisely why I do not trust you with either of my children. The fact that you could even hear a rumor about mistakes of my youth and think that gives you any kind of liberty to excuse anyone's behavior, let alone Abby's or Daniel's, who have been raised better, just shows how completely flawed your judgment is."

"I'm sorry, I didn't mean to imply anything about—"

"Furthermore, you surprise even my already low opinion of you in speaking to an elder and a leader of this community like this."

"Mrs. Mills, I didn't mean— Please, let me explain—"

Whatever thoughts of familial intimacy Caroline might have hoped for were now far from her mind. She didn't think she would lose Daniel over an argument like this, but suddenly she would not be surprised if she did. Mrs. Mills was simply too rigid, too judgmental to be reasoned with.

"This conversation is over." Mrs. Mills stood, as though to put a period on the discussion. "I will not be telling Abby you stopped by to see her. In fact, I want you to forget you ever knew a person named Abigail Mills."

What Caroline was hearing seemed so absurd she thought she must have misunderstood. "I'm sorry, what? What are you saying?"

"I know my son is a grown man and I can't very well stop him from seeing you, but I want you to stay away from my daughter."

"Excuse me?"

"I know you've become friends of a sort. I'm sure it must be very nice for you to have a friend with as many connections and stability as my children have, but I don't trust you to be a good influence on her. I've told her as much as well. She is far too young and too impressionable. I won't have you taking advantage of her."

Caroline's heart pounded in her chest as she listened to Daniel's mother make accusation after accusation.

"Why are you doing this?" she asked quietly.

"Because I know about women like you, Miss Harper. Women who were engaged previously. Women who have no consideration of how their actions appear to those in their community. Many of the young women of Eden Valley look up to you—you are marrying the mayor's son, after all. Think of the model you are setting for them, with your hunting and your disrespect and your requiring everyone around you to drop what they're doing to cater to you."

This last accusation finally fanned the flame of Caroline's ire that she had thus far been able to keep at a smolder. Yes, she knew that she was not nearly as prepared or knowledgeable as most of the other women in this settlement, but for Mrs. Mills to imply—no, to say outright—that she was anything less than a capable adult was infuriating.

Caroline stood, her hands balled into fists at her sides as she struggled to keep her tone level.

"I will grant you that I do not have the connections or background that your children have. That I only learned to do laundry for myself in the last few months and I still ruin some dishes when I cook. I will also gladly admit that I don't have children myself, so I cannot fathom what it must be like to be as afraid as you seem to be all the time that they will be . . ." She cast about for the right word. "Corrupted. But I assure you, both of your children—Abby *and* Daniel—are old enough to know their own minds. They are more than capable of taking care of themselves. Attempting to put restrictions on either of them, especially Abby, will not work the way you want it to. And frankly, Mrs. Mills . . ."

Caroline stopped, unsure if the next sentence that came to mind was worth saying. It wasn't as though she *wanted* to hurt Daniel's mother.

But the smug, knowing look on the older woman's face pushed Caroline's temper over the top. She no longer cared about saving any shred of cordiality they might have had. Maybe what she was about to say would destroy her whole future, but the future that she would have with this woman as her family did not seem worth saving anymore.

"Frankly, Mrs. Mills, I feel sorry for you. You so clearly do not see the reality that is right in front of you, and your grasping for what you wish it was is only putting more and more distance between you and the rest of your family. You are going to end up alone and unhappy if you keep pushing your children away."

Caroline didn't wait for a response. She had nothing more to say and did not care to hear whatever feeble defense the other woman might come up with. She stalked back to the Sullivans' camp, hurt and furious but at the same time petrified she had just lost everything.

CHAPTER THIRTY-ONE

The walk from the Mills family's campsite to the Sullivans' was not more than a couple hundred feet, but to Caroline it seemed as long as the Oregon Trail itself. After arguing so bluntly with Mrs. Mills, Caroline now questioned every decision she had made since she had met that family. She was sure, as she made her way between the wagons, that every family she passed, every man and woman she once counted as a friend, knew of her shame, knew of her rejection and her inability to measure up to that woman's standards.

Caroline almost wondered why she should even bother trying. Maybe Daniel would be better off with someone else. Maybe she should just settle into a life of spinsterhood; Mrs. Sullivan would let her live with them, surely.

The Sullivans' camp, when she reached it, was quiet. The little girls must have been off playing with a friend, and Junior was nowhere to be seen. The campfire smoldered with low embers and the breakfast dishes had been put away.

"Oh, you're back!" Mrs. Sullivan had just climbed out of the wagon. "I didn't expect you until midday at least. I thought you and Abby had much more to do."

Caroline took a deep breath, trying to quell her anger, but the hurt and frustration were too fresh. Her despair was too overwhelming.

"Are you all right?" Mrs. Sullivan asked, approaching cautiously as she peered more closely at Caroline.

She shook her head. Angry tears spilled down her cheeks, but she didn't want anyone's pity. She was too stunned at how that interaction had gone to be anything but angry. Even her hopelessness came with a vein of fury that ran deep. She had worked far too hard to get here to be put through such an insult.

And if she was honest, she felt a little bit sorry for Daniel and Abby. To have grown up with a mother like that. No wonder the younger girl had such a strong desire to build her own income and be free of that home, that dependence on her parents.

"Mrs. Mills asked me not to speak to Abby anymore."

"Oh, honey . . . I'm sorry. That must be so hard. Why would she ask that?"

"And if she thought it would work, she told me that she would ask Daniel not to speak to me anymore either."

That earned a confused expression from Mrs. Sullivan. "Surely she didn't say that."

"She did." Caroline sighed. "And I lost my temper and . . . I told her I was sorry for her, and that . . ." A helpless laugh burst from her throat. "I actually don't remember everything I said. I don't think it was kind, though, or understanding. I lost my temper. And I am halfway expecting Daniel to come over this evening and end our engagement because of how I spoke to his mother, and—and I hope you are all right with me maybe living with you forever, because if Mrs. Mills objects to me, it's probably only a matter of time until every other person in this town goes along with her and I'll be ostracized, but I'll do my best to not embarrass you, if you'll have me."

"Oh, Caroline." Mrs. Sullivan embraced her tightly, securely. In this woman's arms, Caroline learned what her life could have been like if she had grown up with a mother around. She dissolved into tears, wetting the other woman's shoulder.

"I'm sorry," she whispered. "I'll be all right in a minute. It's all just been so much."

"Of course it has. And such ingratitude after you spent all day yesterday helping her daughter." Mrs. Sullivan pulled away, held Caroline by the shoulders so she made eye contact. "That woman would be lucky to have you marry Daniel. Don't let anyone tell you otherwise."

"Thank you." Caroline dried her tears with the cuffs of her sleeve. "I'll be all right. I should find Daniel, maybe. Make sure he hears my side of it before he gets an earful from his mother."

"That might be smart," Mrs. Sullivan agreed. "And that reminds me—there's a note for you. Just there." She pointed to the front of the wagon. "Junior came by while you were gone and left that for you. He didn't say who it was from, but he made me promise that I would make sure you saw it. Maybe it's from Daniel?"

"Oh?"

Caroline crossed to where the folded sheet of paper rested under a small rock, balanced on the wagon seat. She immediately hoped it was from Daniel. True, he had never before written her a note, but that was all the more reason she could hope for a special gesture. She set aside the fact that he could not have heard about her fight with his mother and had time to write such a missive.

She climbed up into the wagon seat and settled in to read. Opening up the note, her first thought was that the handwriting seemed vaguely familiar. As her eyes fell on the first sentence, Caroline realized why she recognized it. A jolt of panic shot through her.

Dear Caroline, it began. *I know when you see what we are asking, you will be more angry than we have ever seen you. Please believe that we wouldn't be asking this if we had any other choice. You are our only friend and our only chance at preserving some happiness with our families once this all comes to light.*

"Oh, no, Abby . . . what have you done?" Caroline murmured as she read on with a sinking feeling.

Abby's steady hand continued. *Tomorrow, I need you to give my parents and Mrs. Sullivan the news. We trust you to do it gently but firmly and help prepare them for when we return. The fact is this: Junior and I are riding to Fort Vancouver tonight to be married by the priest there. Of course, we can't trust that Pastor Montgomery would keep our secret long enough to marry us, but I am sixteen and plenty old enough to know my mind—*

Caroline stopped reading. Abby went on for another couple paragraphs, but whatever further excuses or justifications the girl would give for running away from home to be married would not be worth the time it took Caroline to read them.

All of a sudden Abby's behavior over the previous few weeks had become so clear. Her desire to make money of her own, her seeming lack of concern for what her mother thought about any of her choices, and her clinging to Caroline, the one person who knew her secret. Even her last note about how Caroline wouldn't need to keep the secret much longer.

Caroline wondered how long this elopement had been planned, how much the younger girl had deliberately manipulated her.

A vision of Mrs. Mills's cold, angry face floated into Caroline's mind. As much as that woman claimed to treasure her children, Caroline wasn't at all sure that she would ever forgive her sixteen-year-old daughter for such defiance. If Caroline sat back and let this happen, she could be party to not only an insurmountable rift in the families, but also whatever unhappiness that might grow in a marriage begun on impulse.

And Caroline, through Abby's selfish thoughtlessness, had been dragged into the middle of it.

She had to act.

There was no way of knowing when the couple had left camp, or how far ahead they were. Caroline had no time to waste.

"I have to go," she called to Mrs. Sullivan as she climbed down from the wagon. "I have to— When did you see Junior?"

CHAPTER THIRTY-TWO

"When was Junior here? When did he leave this note?" Caroline shouted to Mrs. Sullivan as she climbed hastily down from the wagon. "Quick—I need to know."

The older woman smiled confusedly at her. "While you were gone. I don't know . . . maybe half an hour? Probably not even that long. Why? What does it say?"

"Was he alone? Which direction did he go?"

Caroline wrung her hands, completely overwhelmed by the disaster that she had been caught in the middle of. That she had no idea how to fix. She was the only one who knew there was a disaster at all. If only she knew how to find Daniel.

But there was no time. It was up to her.

Without a second thought, Caroline climbed into their wagon and collected her warmest shawl, her rifle, and a leather satchel. Into that she packed extra bullets, a knife, and some jerky from the deer Junior had shot only a couple weeks earlier. She hoped against hope that she would be able to find them before they got too far, that she wouldn't be staying overnight anywhere, but she knew she had to be prepared.

There would be no one coming to save her.

When she climbed out of the wagon again, she was confronted by Mrs. Sullivan, still with her confused expression.

"Caroline, what is this about? Is everything all right? What did the note say?"

There was no alternative. She was tired of keeping this secret from the people who most needed to know, especially this woman who had been so kind to her.

"The note was from Abby. She is eloping," Caroline told her, trying to stay calm.

"What?"

"With Junior."

"No! Oh, no, Junior . . . They're just children."

"I'm probably the only person they told. They're on their way to Fort Vancouver and I need to go after them. I'm sure Abby has some . . . misguided idea that this is the only way she can be happy, because of how her mother is. She thinks she needs some dramatic escape."

"And Junior just wants to fix things. He's always been like that. Goodness. Oh, Caroline." Mrs. Sullivan looked around their campsite frantically. "Here—take this canteen. I just filled it. Take . . . I don't know. I don't know what to do."

"I don't either, but I'll do my best. Can you get word to Daniel somehow?"

Without Junior and Hannah to ferry messages around town, with only the littlest girls who needed to be looked after, Mrs. Sullivan had limited options. But they were part of a community. They were surrounded by families who would help.

"Be discrete," Caroline warned. "I don't know that the Millses will thank us for spreading this gossip around. Maybe I can stop it before anything gets worse."

Mrs. Sullivan nodded resolutely. "I know just what to do."

"I'm glad. I don't."

"Yes, you do." Mrs. Sullivan put a calm, strong hand on her arm. "You are capable and smart, Caroline. You have the resources and the courage to fix this. Just do your best. Those two are old enough to live with the consequences of their mistakes, but let's hope it doesn't come to that."

"If I'm not back before dark, it's most likely because I had to go all the way to Fort Vancouver."

Mrs. Sullivan paled, her eyes wide, but she nodded. "If you're not back before dark, you know Daniel will go after you."

"I hope so."

"Godspeed, my dear. Good luck."

With that, Caroline set off toward the north, toward the fort, toward where she hoped she would be able to find signs of Abby and Junior before they did anything irreversible. Behind her, she heard Mrs. Sullivan murmuring to herself, but Caroline had to trust that the woman would be able to take care of what she needed to. She was a worried mother, yes, but she was strong.

Caroline walked rapidly, only hesitating to run because she wasn't certain where she was going yet. As Caroline turned over the situation in her mind, she realized that Abby must have known this was the plan for several days already. Why else would she have told Caroline she wouldn't need to keep the secret much longer?

Caroline also realized that the pair would be riding to Fort Vancouver—each had their own horse, and walking would take days. They could already be well ahead of her. She would need to ride, too, if she was going to have any chance at reaching them. There was one place she knew to go, and now, finally, she started running.

The Kirk family camp was on the far north side of the collection of wagons, and Caroline arrived just as Mr. Kirk was tightening the saddle on Peanut.

"Oh, thank goodness I caught you. Mr. Kirk, I need your horse!" she demanded, huffing from the run. "Please. Peanut. Just for a few hours."

"Ex-excuse me?" He seemed taken aback by her urgency.

"I'm sorry, I don't have time to explain, but I need to, uh—go . . . I need to go after someone, and I don't have my own horse yet to do it, so I was hoping I could borrow yours again, please. Please, Mr. Kirk. I wouldn't ask if it wasn't so important. Remember, I rode Peanut before. She likes me. *Please.*"

"I need my horse, too, Miss Harper. I can't just hand her over on a whim, no matter how important you think it is. Today we had planned to ride out farther, foraging for onions so our store of food can be ready before the first snowfall. Delaying that could mean we don't have enough to eat before spring."

"I understand. I do." She looked over her shoulder, toward the north, as though she could somehow see how far ahead Junior and Abby had gotten. "But what I have to do can only be done right *now*, and if I don't go after them, what happens could be . . . I . . ."

He continued to watch her curiously, seeming to soften when he saw the fear and frustration in her demeanor.

"I can pay!" she finally said, desperately, as she suddenly remembered the gold coin secured in her apron. "Please. I can compensate you for the loss."

Fumbling with the threads that held her apron pocket shut, Caroline withdrew the gold Beaver coin she had been carrying for days. Though her intention had been to save this for her future, or even to help buy a horse of her own, if it now allowed her to stop Abby and Junior it would be money well spent.

He gaped at her, eyeing the gold in her hand.

"Where did you get that?"

"It's not important. I sold something, and now I have this coin to help compensate you for the loss of your horse for the day. It's worth five dollars, Mr. Kirk. Please —*please*—believe me when I tell you I would not be begging like this if I had any other option."

He looked at her skeptically. "I'll take your money and be grateful for it, but Miss Harper, you're not going to last long as a farmer's wife if you think money can take the place of the time you invest in your home."

"Thank you," she gushed, ignoring his criticism. "Oh, thank you so much."

He finished saddling the horse, Caroline growing more impatient as she was so close to finally being off.

"You sure you'll be okay riding her?" he asked as he led the animal to where Caroline waited. "You sure you'll be all right alone? I seem to remember the last time you and Daniel Mills borrowed her you were unsure on your seat. If my Peanut breaks a leg or runs off while you're riding her, that will be far more than the five-dollar coin to replace her."

Caroline nodded quickly, trying to convince herself as well as him. "I can do it, Mr. Kirk. I will be careful, I promise. I just need to be faster than I can walk. I won't take any unnecessary risks."

In answer he just shook his head and handed the reins to her. "You want help up?"

"Please. Thank you. Thank you so much."

In minutes, Caroline had situated herself astride the mare for only the third time in her life. She knew Peanut was calm and an easy seat, but she was still struck by how alone and how unprepared she was for this.

"Good luck," Mr. Kirk said to her.

As she nudged the horse forward and away from camp she called over her shoulder, "I'll be back as soon as I can!"

Peanut knew her way around the trails that curled out from the town, and Caroline allowed the horse to be in charge for the first few minutes while she assessed what she had to do. She had watched Daniel ride off or return home from Fort Vancouver maybe a dozen times, but she only had a vague idea what direction it was in. She had no map, no compass. She had her rifle and a bit of food, but none of it was enough if she had to be gone overnight.

She put that risk from her mind. All she could control right now was moving forward, step by step, as quickly as she could.

Nudging Peanut to go faster, Caroline kept her eyes

on the trail ahead of her. She was no tracker, that was certain, but both Daniel and Junior had taught her a bit of what she could look for when they were hunting. She was riding too fast to be certain, but she thought she noticed fresh horse prints in the soft ground. The grass along the edge of the trail seemed to be newly trampled.

Caroline was completely out of her depth, trying to follow two near-adults who didn't want to be found, but she had to do her best.

Surely Junior and Abby wouldn't be rushing, wouldn't expect pursuit. Surely she could catch up with them—as long as she was going the right way. Oh, why hadn't she asked Daniel more questions about the path to the fort?

Fighting back tears of frustration, Caroline kept an eye on the sun as it rose toward the top of the sky and kept going.

She stopped only once to let Peanut drink from the small stream they passed, but was soon on the trail again. Hours went by, but Caroline refused to let herself feel hopeless. The alternative was giving up, and she wasn't ready to do that just yet.

When the noon sun was high in the sky directly above her, Caroline thought she heard a girl's laughter faintly coming from somewhere ahead of her. Without daring to hope, Caroline urged the mare forward up the low hill to see what lay ahead.

CHAPTER THIRTY-THREE

Nearly two hours passed since Caroline had borrowed the sweet mare from Mr. Kirk. In spite of the late fall weather, the sun above beat a hot, steady drum on the top of her bonnet. The trail she followed was faint, but she kept going, certain that to turn around now would be a bigger mistake than to keep going. As she rode, she wondered what Daniel or Hannah might think of her impulsiveness rushing off into the wilderness by herself. Especially given her inexperience in so many areas. But unlike when she had gone out to her homestead alone, at least this time she had remembered to bring her rifle with her.

All these thoughts were going through Caroline's mind when she finally got a sign that she was close. She heard laughter, far in the distance, and urged her mount ahead.

As she crested a low hill, she spotted two moving figures across the meadow and near the next hill over. Her heart pounded, desperate at the possibility that she had found her quarry. Continuing to ride toward them, Caroline shaded the sun more from her eyes so she could see more clearly. She traveled faster than the figures did, and they became slowly more defined with each foot gained.

When she was within fifty feet, she was sure. This was who she had spent the last couple hours pursuing.

Caroline took a deep breath and yelled as loudly as she could.

"William Sullivan, Junior! Abigail Mills!"

A trio of birds flew up from the bush she passed, startled at the sudden sound. To Caroline's immense relief, the two riders far ahead of her seemed to slow, even stop. She kept riding, urging the mare forward along the narrow trail, eager to catch up to the pair.

As she closed the distance, she heard Junior say her name, confusion evident in his tone.

"Caroline? What . . . how?"

"This is not why I told you!" Abby protested, sounding more like a child than Caroline had ever heard from her.

Junior groaned. "I knew that note was a bad idea."

Caroline drew her horse up alongside them. It was taking all her self-control to not yank Abby right off her own horse and march her back to town.

"Abby Mills, what are you doing? And Junior! I thought better of your judgment than this. Come with me. We're going back, and no one has to know about this ill-thought-out plan."

"No," Abby said defiantly. "No. We're getting married, and then I'll come live with you and not have to deal with my mother anymore, and we'll live happily ever after and have a home of our own one day, and there is nothing you can say that is going to change my mind."

"Oh, no? How about the fact that your mother is ready to write me off completely despite her own beloved son planning to marry me? My offense of . . ." She threw up her hands in frustration. "I don't even know. Being independent? That is nothing compared to you going behind her back like this, let alone what you have planned."

Abby frowned. "What are you talking about?"

Caroline looked around and spotted a wide maple tree not far from them. "Let's go talk, can we?" Abby's horse pulled away before Caroline could try to guide her back to the conversation. "Yelling at each other is only scaring the horses."

"We have to keep going if we're going to get to the fort before dark," Junior said.

Caroline looked at him, her expression a mix of pity and confusion. "Is this really what you want?" she asked softly. "To not have your family at your wedding? To start off your married life with deception and disappointment? You are the man of that family, Junior, and you are disappointing everyone with this choice. Even if you two weren't too young and impulsive to be making this decision, I know that's not the kind of man you are, Junior."

He blushed and ducked his head. He seemed more ashamed than pleased.

Caroline dismounted, letting out the reins a bit so Peanut could rest.

"Please," she said as she looked up to the two

younger people sitting on their horses. "Please come down and talk to me about all this."

They exchanged another look. Abby shook her head, but Junior shrugged. "It's Caroline," he said. "She wouldn't have come all this way if it wasn't important."

"Thank you," Caroline said.

But Abby wasn't moved. "We already decided, Junior. We can't go back now. Changing my mind about this? Mama doesn't need any more reason to think me fickle and flighty."

"No, she'll think you're making a mature decision," Caroline insisted. "Admitting you made a mistake, instead of being stubborn about it—you don't think your mother would love that? Give her the chance to say she was right, even? If you come back with me now, there's still enough time to reach home before dark. Before supper, maybe. And we can all sleep on it tonight and come up with the next step in the morning."

"Abby . . . maybe she has a point?" Junior offered his hand across the space between their horses, reaching for hers. "Maybe we were too hasty. We could have at least told our parents we were going to do this."

"Are you turning on me too, Junior?"

"No!" He looked aghast. "No, of course not. But . . . I just think maybe we should listen to what she has to say."

"Abby," Caroline interjected. "Please trust that I have no intention of hurting you or ruining anything between the two of you. I'm here because I fear that you're not considering all the ramifications of this choice, and what folks—what your parents—will think when they learn about it."

"You showed me that it's okay to not care about what other people think of you." Abby shrugged, as though trying to show she didn't care.

"No, I—"

"I thought that if you still wanted to marry my brother, knowing that Mama might not ever like you, then I could make that same leap."

Caroline groaned. "It is not the same thing at all. Eloping? Why would you think I could be supportive of that?"

"You've always seemed supportive of my other choices. You encouraged me to make the rugs to try to earn an income and be independent of my parents."

"All right, but I never would have encouraged you in your business if I had known the true goal. You were not honest with me about that."

"You told me you would keep our secret when I asked you. You were supportive that whole time!"

"I told you I would keep the secret of you two courting. That is a very, very different thing."

"I love him, Caroline. We love each other. It's the same as you marrying Daniel."

"No. It absolutely is not. You are sixteen. Even if you were a man, that would be far too young to be able to decide you could responsibly have whiskey, let alone tie your life to another person's. Especially a man who has no home of his own either. No offense meant, Junior, but there is a reason the land claims are only available to couples over eighteen years old."

"We could have figured something out."

"Goodness, Abby, you know perfectly well there's a reason you were hesitant to let your mother know about you and Junior in the first place. Don't you think that need for secrecy tells you something?"

"I don't know what you mean."

Caroline looked hard at her, sensing the doubt behind her defiance. She wanted so badly to get through to the younger girl, but Abby had that tendency to rebellion and Caroline was afraid she might push her too far.

"You trusted me, remember? Please continue to trust me. I'm not letting you two make this mistake. If you both decide you are still in love and still want to get married once you have come clean with all of your family members and are not sneaking around in secrecy, I will be the first one to show up at your wedding. But right now, making this enormous decision under such deceptive circumstances? I would be no friend to you if I hung back and let you do this, to say nothing of what your families would think of me."

They looked at each other. Caroline could already tell that Junior had softened, but that boy was always so happy to keep the peace she wasn't sure she could trust his conviction.

"Please," Caroline continued more gently. "I may be able to justify the apparently unladylike job of hunting, even if some folks look down on me, but I still value the opinions and respect of people like Mrs. Sullivan or Daniel—or your father, you know? He's a good man. And this would hurt him so much."

"She's right, Abby," Junior said softly. "Ma already lost my father and my brother. I can't do this to her. It's not right. I can't hurt her like this."

Abby's nostrils flared with a surge of anger, but it

quickly dissipated. "But what about my mother? What am I supposed to do about her?"

The proud defiance had left her tone, and Caroline could see that she was in real pain. Whatever judgment Mrs. Mills had leveled against Caroline was nothing compared to the standards to which she held her own daughter. Abby may have been flippant about the criticism, but deep down every young woman wants her mother's approval.

Caroline swallowed hard. She had to be honest with the girl.

"I don't know, Abby. I'm sorry. We can talk to her, talk to Daniel, maybe even ask the pastor to talk to her. But it might take time. And it will probably be hard to get her to understand you. What I do know, though, is that your relationship with your mother will only get worse if you run away to get married in secret. That's something you can never come back from, and I don't think you want to give up all hope of having your parents in your life . . . do you?"

Abby bit the inside of her cheek as she listened and thought.

"I don't want to be alone," she said finally, tears in her eyes.

"You will never be alone," Caroline said with conviction, fully aware that she was repeating the very same thing Hannah had said to her many times. "So many people love you, including your mother in her own way. And we'll bring her around to all of this, and you and Junior can marry in a couple years once things are more settled."

Abby and Junior shared another look, shy smiles on both their faces.

"I love you, Abby. I love you like a sister, like I love Junior as though he was my own younger brother. Please believe that this is the best thing for you. Now please come home with me."

Not taking her eyes from Junior, Abby finally nodded. "Yes. All right."

CHAPTER THIRTY-FOUR

Though it had taken some convincing from both Caroline and Junior, finally Abby had admitted that running away to get married was not the mature, well-thought-out choice that she had hoped it would be. She agreed to return to Eden Valley that afternoon, though it was clear she wasn't happy about it. Caroline tried not to let on how grateful she was that she had been able to change the other girl's mind. Instead, she kept the conversation focused on the future and the changes they could make.

The trio rode back to Eden Valley far more slowly than they had left it. They had spent hours riding toward the fort, and now had to spend hours more riding back. Caroline wanted to be considerate of Peanut, given how hard she had ridden to get her there. At the same time, she wanted to be mindful of the emotions and disappointment of the couple she was escorting. They were having to reassess their next steps.

"You'll have time to build a home and plan out a new

dress or whatever else you might want for your wedding," Caroline reminded her. "You'll be able to do it all exactly the way you want so there are no regrets."

"That's assuming we actually get to talk. Mama will never let me see him again," Abby grumbled. "I'll never forgive you for this, Caroline Harper."

Caroline didn't respond right away. She remembered her own dramatics and heartache when she had been Abby's age, so sure that she knew everything and that anyone who opposed her was her enemy. She trusted that with time Abby would see the value in what Caroline was offering them.

"I'm sure it won't be that dire. Especially not forever. Forever is a long time."

Abby snorted a laugh. "You sound like Pa."

Caroline grinned. "I certainly did not expect to be this old and wise even when so young."

"Ha-ha," Abby responded without emotion.

"It will work out, Abby," Junior added for the fifth time. "You'll see. I promise. As soon as I turn eighteen, I'll claim a homestead and start building our home."

"So, um . . ." Caroline began, as they rode side by side. "I have been wondering about that. What exactly were your plans before I stopped you? How were you going to live?"

"Junior said we could just stay with his mother."

"Oh, he did, did he?" Caroline looked at the young man.

Junior blushed but raised his chin to the challenge. "I figured if Ma was okay with you living there she'd be okay with Abby too. Especially now that Hannah's gone."

"So you were . . . what? Going to have your wife sleep in the wagon with your mother and sisters? Or, better yet, have her sleep in the tent outside with you? In this weather?"

The look of horror on Abby's face made Caroline laugh.

"Didn't get that far in your plans, did you?" she suggested.

"Maybe it is better if we wait," Abby admitted, riding closer to Junior. "Don't you dare tell anyone I said that though, Caroline. I will play the heartbroken, lovelorn youth to perfection, to stoke Mama's sympathy and get her on my side as soon as possible."

"Abby." Caroline shook her head. "Just be honest with her. Trying to manipulate her feelings is just going to end you up in the same impossible situation you've been in."

"And is that what you do?" she challenged. "You've been in just as an impossible situation, haven't you? I seem to recall you coming to me for tips on how to handle her, instead of being honest with Mama after all her criticism and assumptions."

Caroline remembered the conversation—the argument—she'd had with Mrs. Mills just that morning. She had finally been honest with her . . . and had regretted it in the immediate aftermath.

"I have been honest with her, yes," she responded finally. She went on to offer Abby the broad strokes of how she and her mother had argued that morning. About how hard it was for her, and about how she thought she could be risking everything. Junior listened quietly, grimacing at the harsher aspects of the conversation, sympathetic as ever.

"But I realized," she concluded, "that if I continued to try to be someone I'm not just to make that woman happy, there would be nothing left for me to make me happy. And . . . it was scary. And I still don't know how it will all play out. I came after you immediately afterward."

"What will you do if she is able to convince my brother not to marry you?"

Caroline shrugged. "Something else, I suppose. I don't know. If Daniel comes to me tomorrow, for example, and tells me that he doesn't want . . ." She cleared her throat and composed herself. "That he can't marry me, then I'll just figure something else out. I don't know. But I have to live with myself first, and that means being true to how I feel."

"Yes," Abby said softly.

"And you're going to need to live with yourself. If starting a rug-making business makes you happy, then you should do it. If you love Junior enough to marry him, then you must love him enough to wait until the right time. But if you're doing either of those things to escape or spite your mother, there must be a better way to spend your energy."

Abby looked at Caroline for a long moment before offering her what seemed to be a sad smile and changing the subject.

"How long, do you think, until Dr. Martell's home is finished?"

Junior seemed a bit taken aback by the shift, but he launched into an animated description of what gossip and priorities he had heard in the previous days, which public buildings would be completed in the spring. Caroline grinned, watching him describe the forthcoming schoolhouse and his evident pride at the fact that he would no longer be attending when it was done.

Finally, after riding all day, they reached the north end of Eden Valley about an hour before sunset, and Caroline guided them to the Kirk camp. She returned Peanut to Mr. Kirk with effusive gratitude. His confused expression when he saw who she was with was ignored, and the three continued on to the campsite where most of the families in town remained.

As Abby and Junior walked their horses slowly to keep pace with Caroline, the sounds and smells of supper over campfires spread through the landscape all around them. As more homes were completed, more of the campfire meals were replaced by roasting venison in a fireplace or long, slow batches of stew that could cook all day. The flickering light of fires out in the open was slowly being replaced by the dim, steady light of a lamp from within a cabin. Eden Valley was slowly becoming the established home they had all hoped for.

The Sullivans' camp was the next closest, and Caroline felt herself getting nervous as they approached. She realized now that she hadn't stayed long enough to really know how the boy's mother felt about it all.

But as soon as they were noticed, Caroline relaxed.

"Junior!"

Mrs. Sullivan rushed forward, catching her only remaining son in her arms the moment he had dismounted.

"Thank you for coming home," she whispered to

him. "I'm so glad you're back. I was so worried. Don't you ever do that to me again. I'm so glad you're back."

"It's okay, Ma," he said, patting her back. "It's all right."

"Say goodbye," Caroline prompted Abby. "I'm walking you to your own camp."

Junior and Abby said a shy goodbye—the first time they had actually been noticed together by any of their friends or family—and made promises to speak the following day. Caroline could see from the look on Mrs. Sullivan's face that that might not be the case, but if Caroline knew her, she'd relent soon.

Caroline didn't interrupt, but the moment they stepped apart she guided Abby to the other side of camp and her own family.

"Good luck," she murmured as the pair drew closer to the younger girl's judgment. She could see the trepidation in Abby's face, an uncertainty that she rarely revealed. "Do you want me to stay?"

Abby shook her head. "No, I need to deal with this. You're right, and being honest with Mama is the only thing that might actually get us through this with a relationship on the other side. I can do it. I think. I can try, at least."

The two were only a dozen feet away from the campfire when Mrs. Mills finally noticed them. She looked up before standing abruptly, staring at her returned daughter. Caroline couldn't read the expression on Mrs. Mills's face. And she didn't try. There was no knowing how much the older woman knew, what Mrs. Sullivan or Daniel had told her. And there was no telling how she felt now about Caroline after all that had happened that day.

But Abby wanted to handle this on her own.

Mr. Mills approached then, coming from the meadow where his cattle grazed just beyond the wagons. He opened his arms for one of the big, heartfelt hugs he was known for.

"Abigail," he said gently.

Caroline backed away in the growing dusk and left the Mills family alone.

CHAPTER THIRTY-FIVE

Caroline returned to the Sullivan camp absolutely depleted in mind and body. Mrs. Sullivan had sent the little girls to bed early and was sitting talking intently to Junior when Caroline got back. She merely nodded in acknowledgment and climbed into the wagon to go to bed. Too much of Caroline's day had already been spent handling other people's problems; what she wanted most right now was to rest and let Junior worry about Junior.

Most of the following day, Caroline busied herself with all the chores and tasks she had been ignoring for the previous forty-eight hours. Though her mind was with Abby and her mother—as well as what it could all mean for her own place in the Mills family—she was careful to keep her hands and body busy. She tried not to interrupt or impose on the Sullivans' family reunion either, reminding herself that, depending on what happened, she might be alone like this more and more often.

Junior easily settled back into the day-to-day labor of

helping build the remaining houses for the frontier town. The cabin the men were building for Mrs. Sullivan and the children was close to being done, and the young man seemed eager to do his part.

"I think he feels guilty," Mrs. Sullivan confided to Caroline that afternoon. "If he had gone off and married without telling me while leaving me without a roof over our heads?" She laughed. "That boy is too sweet for his own good sometimes. He's bound to be taken advantage of."

"Not that you're complaining that he returned," Caroline prodded.

"No, I'm not," she said, serious again. "And if I ever stop thanking you for going after them, you can assume my mind has gone. I don't know what either of them was thinking, and I don't rightly know what we would have done without you. Guess I gotta keep my eye on him a little bit longer."

Such praise both embarrassed and pleased Caroline. As she hadn't heard a word from either Daniel or Mrs. Mills, she kept vacillating back and forth between whether or not her choices the previous day had been right. Knowing Mrs. Sullivan was grateful was helpful, but Caroline couldn't forget the fact that she had specifically interfered in Abby's life when her mother had asked her not to. But she pushed it from her mind as best she could. What was done was done.

Patience and Martha had not been told what was happening the day before, and were full up with questions, sensing a change in their brother. When the little girls asked about it, however, Mrs. Sullivan redirected their curiosity to the new home that was due to be completed soon.

"Do I get my own room?" Martha said when her mother asked if she was excited.

"No, love, but you will have a real bed soon. And a floor, and a roof made of something other than canvas."

"Will I still be able to hear the crickets and things when I fall asleep?"

Mrs. Sullivan exchanged an amused look with Caroline.

"No, probably not."

"Aw, Ma. Then I don't want to move."

"Maybe," Caroline offered, "in the summer when it's warm enough, your brother will camp outdoors with you again and you can fall asleep with the bugs."

"Yuck! Bugs!" Patience added.

"Bugs," a familiar voice called. "I leave for a day and you resort to eating bugs?"

"Hannah!" Martha and Patience shouted their sister's name together and ran to hug her.

"What about you?" Hannah called to Caroline over the little girls' heads. "Are you going to come hug me, or are you still mad that I deserted you?"

"I didn't think we would see you here for weeks," Caroline said as she too crossed to hug her friend.

"Daniel told Ben about what happened," she said in a low voice after sending the girls off to play. "I wanted to make sure everything was all right. Goodness, Caroline . . . I wouldn't have thought it of Junior. And I can't believe you went after them!"

"You kind of expected something like this from Abby though, huh?" Caroline joked.

"Goodness," Hannah said again with a chuckle. "Maybe."

As they sat down and Caroline filled her friend in on all she had been through over the previous couple days, she marveled all over again that she'd had the courage to ride off into the wilderness, let alone everything else.

"And what does Daniel say?" Hannah asked.

"I haven't, um . . . I haven't seen him. Your mother had Caleb find and send word to him yesterday, and apparently he talked to Ben? But I haven't seen him."

"Oh, well, I'm sure there's a good reason for that."

"Maybe. Or maybe his mother got to him, and he's just trying to figure out a way to tell me."

"Don't think like that."

"Anyway. Enough about me. How's married life? How is it having an actual door again?"

"I wish it were spring so we could get started on all the projects and kitchen garden I have in mind for our farm," Hannah said, her eyes twinkling. "I know winter will be a good chance to lay in and get ahead on things like sewing, but you know I don't do so well with sitting still."

"I have good news for you then. There is always plenty to do here."

Hannah stayed with her family through the afternoon, playing with the little girls and helping her mother make a big batch of stew from one of the rabbits Junior had hunted just that morning.

"I see what you mean by him feeling guilty," she said as she cut up an onion. "After the day he had yesterday, today getting up before dawn to hunt and then going off to build a house?" She shook her head in wonder.

"If he asks," Mrs. Sullivan said, "make sure to tell him I'm still heartbroken over it."

"Patience, come here and stir for me, please," Hannah said. "Be careful of the flames and your skirt. Now that I'm gone, you girls are going to have to help more."

"At least until your brother gets married and brings a wife here to help out too," Mrs. Sullivan said slyly.

"Ma!" Hannah exclaimed.

"Who is he going to marry?" Patience asked innocently.

"Oh, heavens," Mrs. Sullivan said with a laugh. "Forget I said anything."

Caroline hung back, happy to watch her best friend interacting with her family. This might be all Caroline had in the years to come, and if nothing else she was very grateful for the love and humor and genuine friendship between members of the Sullivan family. She couldn't have asked for a better one.

When Martha started asking how she could help, Caroline turned away to fetch more firewood. She hadn't gotten more than a few steps when Daniel appeared, striding down the path from the direction of the Mills family's camp.

"Why, if it isn't Mr. Mayor Junior?" Hannah said.

Daniel offered a wave to the group before resting his eyes on Caroline. "I won't keep you long. I see you have a guest." Hannah curtsied. "But can I talk to you quickly?"

Caroline's heart beat wildly, but Daniel seemed calm enough. Maybe she needn't have worried quite so much. "Come help me find more firewood?" she suggested.

They walked out past the edge of the camp, toward where broken branches and felled trees had been collected as the town went up. Caroline began to pick up some of the more likely looking pieces, while Daniel followed.

"My mother wants to come talk to you."

Caroline let out a little gasp.

"And . . . given everything," he continued, "I told her I would check with you to make sure that was acceptable before she does."

She frowned. "Really?"

"I'm not sure exactly what she wants to say. She wouldn't tell me. But I do get the impression that she . . . she knows what she could have lost."

Caroline nodded thoughtfully.

"But if you don't want to see her, Caro, I will tell her that. There's nothing she can say to me that will make me leave your side."

Tears welled up, and Caroline was surprised by the strength of her feeling of gratitude.

"Thank you," she whispered. "I would like it if she and I could make up . . . somehow. I don't know what to say to her, but I can listen."

"I'll tell her tomorrow, shall I?" he said, looking over Caroline's shoulder to where the Sullivan family was gathered for supper. "Once Hannah has gone."

"I really appreciate you, Daniel."

"We'll get through this, Caro."

She nodded.

"Now, let me get some of this firewood for you. You've not grabbed more than one meal's worth."

CHAPTER THIRTY-SIX

Daniel helped her bring more firewood and then said his goodbyes. Caroline fretted a bit after he left, but having Hannah around helped. She hadn't fully admitted to herself how much she had missed her friend, and was grateful for her presence. When Ben came to collect her after supper, the two women made promises for Caroline to visit soon.

"Please don't make me keep cleaning this house just for him," Hannah said, nudging her husband playfully. "I need a guest."

After Hannah left, and after the little girls went to bed, Caroline confided in Mrs. Sullivan what Daniel had come by to ask her.

"And how do you feel?"

"Anxious," Caroline admitted. "Not as much as I was before I knew she wanted to talk to me, but still a little bit afraid of what she is going to say. It can't be all bad, right? She wouldn't have sent Daniel to make such a request if she was just going to be cruel about it, would she?"

"I can't imagine she would, no. You know, you would think, with both of our husbands leading the wagon company across the territories, that June Mills and I would have become better friends, but she's always been a bit distant. I can't predict what she might do or think. But I can tell you that as a mother, I am more grateful to you for pounding sense into my son than I will ever be able to repay you for. She might feel the same way."

Caroline nodded, looking into the campfire as it slowly died down to low embers.

"I'm going to bed," Mrs. Sullivan said. She stood and put a hand on Caroline's shoulder. "Will you be all right?"

"I just want to sit a bit longer. I won't be late."

"No matter what happens, dear, remember that we are always here for you."

"I know. Thank you. Good night."

Once she was alone, Caroline poked at the embers a couple times, watching the tiny flames flare before dying again. She leaned back and looked up at the stars, spread generously across the night sky. She closed her eyes and listened to the sounds of the livestock lowing all around her, owls in the distance.

Sitting alone for close to an hour while the fire finished dying, Caroline tried to remind herself of the steady, dependable foundation of love she had all around her. Like the reliability of the night sky, she had Daniel's love and the Sullivans' companionship. No matter what happened the following day with Mrs. Mills, she would be fine. If her wild adventure going after Abby and

Junior had taught her anything, it was that she could do what was necessary, no matter what it was.

The next morning, after breakfast, Mrs. Sullivan took the little girls to a morning reading class with Miss Atkins, while Junior again strode off in the early morning light to put the finishing touches on the next of the cabins to be completed. Caroline knew that Daniel's mother would be coming to see her some time that day, and the anticipation of that moment so distracted her that she could barely focus. She busied herself collecting armful after armful of firewood, even borrowing the Hatchleys' saw to help cut down some of the larger pieces.

If her body was busy, her mind wouldn't be quite so.

She was so successful in this endeavor to distract herself that, as she was returning to camp with several heavier branches, Caroline was surprised to see Mrs. Mills step out from around the side of one of the wagons.

"Miss Harper."

Caroline halted, a wave of fear going over her at the sight of her visitor. Though she had been expecting it all morning, seeing this woman standing in front of her nevertheless brought back all the feelings of uncertainty that had dominated Caroline's thoughts over the last several days.

"Hello. Um . . . let me just set these down."

She had spent the previous days on edge, waiting for whatever verdict Mrs. Mills would lay down. It didn't matter how much Daniel had reassured her last night. It didn't matter how safe she felt with her betrothed. The fact was she had almost certainly hurt the feelings of his mother, before then inserting herself irrevocably in Abby's life after being commanded to do the opposite. She couldn't even guess what the other woman must be feeling, and now she stood here asking for Caroline's attention.

Caroline dropped the firewood by the wagon's back wheel with the other small pieces she had collected and looked around, but the Sullivans had yet to return. Daniel was, of course, elsewhere. Hannah had gone home the night before and wouldn't return for at least another week. Even Abby had been silent, not communicating with Caroline at all since she had brought her home.

She was on her own.

She had to face the consequences with June Mills the best she could.

"Yes, um . . . hello." She cleared her throat. "Can I . . . would you like to sit, or . . . can I get you anything?"

She was rambling and she knew it, but she was afraid if she allowed silence to fall between them then she would be opening herself up to whatever criticism Mrs. Mills had brought with her.

"I brought you this."

The older woman thrust out a small basket to Caroline, awkwardly but not ungraciously. In it was something covered in a linen napkin, protected from the elements.

"Oh. Oh, well, thank you."

She took the proffered basket and looked under the linen that had been folded over. A dozen cinnamon doughnuts had been stacked neatly within, and Caroline could smell that warm, fresh scent that indicated they were freshly fried, exactly as Mrs. Mills had made to help woo potential voters.

And now they were being offered to Caroline.

"Goodness. Thank you," she said again.

When she looked back up in the older woman's face, her expression of sorrow and humility was unmistakable. Caroline softened.

"Oh, won't you please be seated, Mrs. Mills. Please be comfortable. Share one of these with me."

"Well. Yes, all right."

There was a small spindle chair and an overturned bucket across from each other at the smoldering campfire, and Caroline pulled her own seat closer to the other. She set the basket down on the ground between the seats, reached in for one of the doughnuts, and sat up again, waiting.

"This smells amazing," she ventured, before breaking off a small piece. "How kind of you to bring them to me."

Mrs. Mills said nothing, but picked up the basket and put it in her own lap. She folded back the fabric, chose a doughnut, and folded it closed again, but didn't return the basket. Caroline watched her curiously, without judgment but also without knowing quite how to handle the situation.

They sat in silence for a full minute, Caroline eating slowly while Mrs. Mills seemed to be staring off into the distance.

"I wanted to apologize to you, Miss Harper," the older woman said abruptly. She stopped fingering the towel in the basket, straightened her shoulders, cleared her throat, and looked directly at her. "Caroline. My dear. I am so sorry."

Even though she'd suspected this might be coming, Caroline still didn't know what to say. The arrogance of this proud woman had all but disappeared in the wake of her daughter's near-defection.

"I'm sorry too—"

"No, please." Mrs. Mills placed the basket of dough-nuts on the ground again between them and turned to face Caroline. "After you brought Abby home the other night, I was . . . I was so furious, absolutely certain that it was your fault she had left at all. She told me that you had been the only one who knew their secret, and I had an idea in my mind already of what kind of person you were and what you might do. I had already decided I wouldn't stand for you to be in our lives when Daniel came home."

Caroline stayed quiet, sensing that if Mrs. Mills was interrupted she might never again have the courage to say these things.

"Daniel heard my scolding. George was with him, and . . . I've been married nearly thirty years, and George says he has never seen me that angry. He was so worried. And he was right to be. I was so angry it was like I couldn't see straight. The two of them had to get between Abby and me." She shook her head in wonder. "I don't know what might have happened if they hadn't come home when they did. I could have said something I could never take back."

Caroline nodded.

"And once I had calmed myself, Abby explained to me that that was exactly why she had come back and not gone on to Fort Vancouver. She told me that *you* are the reason. That you showed her that eloping, in secret, that hurting her family like that, would be something she could never take back. I'm sure Junior had a hand in convincing her too. I know he is a sweet boy, even if he is far too young to be thinking about getting married. But Abby made sure I knew it was you."

Caroline smiled. "I did my best."

"And I can't thank you enough. I could have lost my daughter. She might never have come back to Eden Valley, let alone speak to me."

"Oh, you can't think like that."

"She told me that," Mrs. Mills said matter-of-factly. She nodded, emphasizing her point. "She was finally honest with me. She told me about the rugs for the general store. She told me that . . ." She choked up, waited a beat, and composed herself before continuing. "She told me that she would rather sleep in a bedroll under the Sullivans' wagon than stay in my home any longer, and . . . I didn't know. I had no idea how unhappy she was. I was just trying to raise her to be the desirable, proper woman I know she can be. But all I was doing was holding her back and pushing her away."

"I know. I think, deep down, Abby knows too. That you were just doing your best."

She nodded. "I hope so. Of course, I know you and Daniel have discussed this, as well as you and Abby, and I just . . . I cannot tell you enough how grateful I am to you and how you have been a support to my children. I know that I have not . . . I haven't appreciated your full worth thus far, and I hope you can forgive me. I'm trying. I'd like if we could be . . . friendly? At least. Since you'll soon be a member of the family."

A grin broke across Caroline's face. "Won't you please share a donut with me, Mrs. Mills?"

The other woman offered a tentative smile in return and accepted the gift.

CHAPTER THIRTY-SEVEN

"We're putting the roof on the general store today," Junior said importantly. "Then some of the men will work on building shelving and a counter for the interior, and hopefully by spring we can send a whole wagon or two to Fort Vancouver for supplies."

The weather was getting colder toward the end of November, and Caroline had taken to wearing three shawls. She wanted to put off using her brother's heavy coat as long as she could, knowing that she had no other warm clothing to don once it actually snowed. Daniel had been trying to explain to her how different snow was in the wilderness than she would have experienced growing up in New York City, but she wasn't sure she understood. Each time she had reminded him that there were several blocks of green and city park to be snowed on, he had just chuckled and told her she would see.

"And then, after the store, it's our home, right?" Mrs. Sullivan asked, with one arm around her youngest daughter. "I've been promised that I won't have to sleep in these wagons through the winter. Please tell me that is still the case."

He grinned. "Might be sooner than you think."

Ever since Caroline had brought Junior and Abby back from their failed elopement, the young man had been a model son, rising before dawn and working wherever he was needed until his mother finally made him sit down to supper. Caroline had an idea that he would be angling to court Abby properly any day now, and thus wanted to shore up his reputation before then.

All of her efforts to interrupt Abby and Junior's elopement had been exciting and stressful, making a return to the everyday tasks of laundry—always more laundry—and cooking an unlooked-for respite. But without Hannah around, there was plenty of work to do, and Caroline was happy to keep herself busy as she waited patiently for her home to be finished. Daniel had promised and hinted that it would be soon, and she was glad to have more mundane things to fill her days in the meantime.

A day later, Caroline was invited to have Sunday supper with the Mills family, and though the meal started out awkward, soon all the members of the family warmed to her. Abby all but lit up when she launched into her plan for how many braided rugs she would be able to make over the winter.

Day after day, Caroline did her work, watched for Daniel, and offered her best to the family that had effectively adopted her. Her patience finally paid off when Junior came home early one afternoon to announce that the Sullivans' home was finally done.

With all that had happened in the previous days, the

end of November seemed to sneak up on Caroline. Weeks earlier, Ben Findley had brought back word from the fort that they couldn't expect any snow until the middle of December, and at the time that had seemed such a long way away. Now though, as Caroline woke in the chilly interior of the Sullivans' wagon, she realized how little time she actually had.

In the previous few days, Martha and Patience had taken to curling up next to Caroline and Mrs. Sullivan as they slept. They had piled their cots with all the blankets they had on hand, but the nights were becoming so cold as to be almost unbearable. But today was moving day, and the Sullivans would be transferring all of their things that had made it to the territories from back east into the cozy, much warmer one-room cabin that had finally been built.

Caroline nudged Martha, rousing her out of a deep sleep, and whispered, "Get up, sunshine. Today is the day!"

Since the wagon company had arrived in the Oregon Territory nearly two months earlier, most of the oxen that had hauled the wagons westward had had a chance to rest and fatten up again. Though not all of the animals had survived long enough to land on this side of the mountains, plenty had, including all of the Sullivans' animals. The enormous creatures seemed confused to be hitched up to the wagons again after so long roaming in the grassland nearby, but by late morning, Junior, Jasper Stephens, and Josiah Hatchley, with some help from Caroline, had the two Sullivan wagons starting down the trail toward the new homestead.

Hannah had come over early to help make sure

everything was in place and her sisters were taken care of, and Caroline walked with them behind the two wagons.

The new Sullivan home was almost a mile from the center of Eden Valley, and as they walked, Hannah told Caroline all about her evenings after supper, with Ben home, and all the plans they'd talked over before bed. Everything, from vegetables to plant in the spring, to delicate needlepoint supplies Hannah wanted to order from back east.

"I suppose one of these days a little one might come along, and I just want to make sure the home is as finished as it can be before that day comes," she concluded, brimming with energy as ever.

She tried to be happy for her friend; Hannah being happily married and settled didn't take anything away from her, after all. But with all the excitement of the day, Caroline was reminded all over again that she didn't have a home of her own. She would always have a place with the Sullivans, but the idea of sleeping on a mat on the floor of a one-room cabin just made her sad.

As the wagons approached the Sullivan home, Caroline recognized the tall figure of Daniel Mills standing near the front door, and he seemed to be waiting for them.

For her.

"Are you here to help?" she asked.

"Yes, but only so you can be done sooner and come with me."

"Go on," Hannah told her. "I'll make Josiah stay, and we'll have plenty of hands. By the time you return everything will be settled."

Caroline didn't argue and eagerly followed Daniel. He had his own horse and had borrowed Abby's for the afternoon, and they rode out farther following a narrow trail. Though they didn't speak much, Caroline had no need for words. She was too happy to be with him, to be moving into a cabin—even if it was temporary—and to finally be on the other side of the stress and secrets that had occupied her for weeks.

After riding for no more than fifteen minutes, Caroline looked around in surprise. She recognized this landscape, that creek. She recognized this part of the settlement. Daniel led them into a stand of trees and dismounted.

Looking at him with excitement, she asked, "Is this . . . Daniel, are we home?"

"Look for yourself."

He took her reins, helped her down, and gestured for her to go on.

Caroline walked through the stand of trees excitedly, anticipation driving her forward.

She gasped.

In the clearing before the next stand of trees was a finished one-room cabin, complete with a stone chimney on the far side.

Caroline whirled on him.

"Daniel Mills. Why didn't you tell me it was so close to being done?"

"You know, we've already been through so much, and the timeline has changed many times. And then you were busy with all the things with Abby. I just thought this would be better as a surprise. Was that all right?" He reached for her hand and stepped closer to her. "Surprise!" he added teasingly.

"It's done, though? It's finished? Can we go inside?"

"Come with me."

Daniel led her across the grass to the front door while Caroline took in all the details she could see. She couldn't help but compare this home with the fine, brick, decades-old townhouses of her friends in New York City. What would they think to see her now? Her home in the Oregon Territory was logs, primarily, with only the most rugged wooden step leading up to the front door. It was bigger than the wagon she had been living in for months, but not by much.

Daniel reached forward and pushed the door open before stepping back to allow Caroline to walk through. The interior was dark—even more so than the interior of the covered wagons—but directly across from the door was a small window cut out of the logs. On the wall to the right was an empty fireplace, and the wall to the left held one long shelf at about the height of Caroline's head.

Daniel took her hand again as he stepped inside next to her. "Don't worry, Caro. I know it's not much, but I have all kinds of plans. We'll work together to make this the home that we want it to be. We'll keep a blanket over the window for now. I think I'll have a chance to travel to the fort and get glass for it in the next couple weeks. If not maybe waxed paper in the meantime? We'll have to see. The bed will go here, under the shelf"—he pointed—"and Bill Alden is almost done building it for me. As soon as I have time I'll make a table and chairs, and then we can decide together what's next."

She could hear the trepidation in his voice, the hope and desperation that she would like all the work that he had done for them.

The home was a blank slate, an empty box just waiting for them to fill it up with their love and their life together.

"I love it. It's perfect. I love it so much."

Tears welled up in her eyes as she felt the overwhelming wave of love and gratitude for this man and this life they would build together.

"Let's get married," Daniel whispered to her as he drew her close. "Day after tomorrow."

CHAPTER THIRTY-EIGHT

Caroline was trembling, she was so happy. Today was finally the day she had been looking forward to. The very end of November, a dark, overcast sky, but enough joy and sunshine in her heart to carry her.

"Is that what you're wearing?" Hannah Findley asked.

"Not all of us get a brand new blue silk dress to be married in."

The two women were in Caroline and Daniel's home, the door thrown open to let in as much light as possible as Caroline assessed herself in the small, narrow mirror her friend had brought over. Her forest-green dress brought out the red tints in her hair, and she was pleased to have gotten the oil stain out of the flounce on the side.

Hannah laughed. "No criticism meant. I was just thinking if we could find flowers that go with that color we could weave some into your hair. What do you think —maybe a pine bough?"

Caroline chuckled and turned back to the small

mirror. Her pale face, framed by auburn hair, dominated the small reflection, the collar of her gown just peeking up. She took a step back, rising onto her toes to see more of the dress. It was one that she had managed to make last through the final weeks traveling on the trail. Worn and old as it was, it was still her best dress. Though she now had several gold coins tucked away, Caroline hadn't wanted to spend the precious funds on a gown. Not when she had several that would work well enough. That was money she could spend on something more practical, like a big stock pot or pigs.

Her wedding day would be one day; her married life would be forever.

"I don't need them," Caroline said. "As long as all my ends are tucked in and there are no stains visible, I am perfectly happy to wed Daniel just as I am. Which, may I remind you, is *not* what I had to look forward to in New York." She turned back to Hannah with a wide grin. "I tried to talk him into just heading to the pastor's house a couple days ago, the minute I knew the house was finished, but he said his mother would never let us hear the end of it."

"And *I* wouldn't have either! I've been waiting for this day just as long as you have."

"Well, now I suppose neither of us have to wait much longer."

"Speaking of . . ." Hannah turned toward the open door. "I think I hear folks. You stay here, I'll go see."

Caroline was left alone in the dimly lit home.

She turned back to the small mirror, looking herself in the eyes. This woman standing in front of her had been through so much. The heartbreak of having to leave the home she'd always known, the frustration of learning all new skills to merely survive, the confusion of having to fight for Mrs. Mills's approval. But she had gotten through all of it, every step of the way. At times her friends and people who loved her had all but carried her, but now Caroline Harper-soon-to-be-Mills stood on her own two feet, in a home where she would live with a husband who cherished her.

Though this was not the life she had envisioned for herself when she was a little girl, now there was nowhere else she would rather be.

"It's time," Hannah called to her from the doorway.

Caroline checked her hair one last time before turning to meet her groom.

The interior of her cabin had been so dark that when Caroline stepped out of the doorway, the brightness of the outdoors blinded her for a moment. As her eyes adjusted, the first thing she saw was Daniel's handsome face smiling at her from a dozen feet away. Though she knew there must be other people gathered there, Caroline only had eyes for him.

She crossed the short distance to where Daniel stood with the pastor and faced him as he took her hands in hers.

The wedding ceremony itself was brief but beautiful. Caroline prayed that she would remember every detail as long as she lived, every word promising her love to Daniel and his in turn to her. This day was the end of such a long journey—but also the beginning of another.

"May your love be a blessing and an example to all who know you. Remember that every marriage is a journey, through good times and bad. May the vows you make today carry you through the rest of your life."

Caroline beamed at Daniel; she felt as though she could float completely up into the air, so elated was she to be committing her life to this man.

Pastor Montgomery pronounced them husband and wife.

When they kissed to seal their love and promise to each other, Caroline felt as though she could simply melt into his arms. The sounds of cheering and applause from their families brought her back down to earth.

"I love you," Daniel whispered, then together they turned toward their guests.

Hannah rushed up to hug her, with Mrs. Sullivan, the little Sullivan girls, and Abby close behind. Caroline laughed as she was crushed in a mass of arms and exclamations.

As those closest to her dispersed, into the gap stepped Daniel's mother. She had just embraced her son, congratulating him on his marriage, and now turned to her new daughter.

"Welcome to the family, dear," Mrs. Mills said, looking Caroline deep in the eyes. "I know that we had a rocky start, but I should have trusted that Daniel would choose a woman who would be the perfect fit for him. I'm grateful you haven't held my past behavior against me."

"Yes, welcome!" Mr. Mills said heartily. He nudged his wife aside to catch up Caroline in a rib-crushing hug. Caroline laughed as she was practically lifted off her feet by the big man.

"George," his wife scolded gently. "Don't hurt the poor girl."

Looking over his shoulder at Daniel, Caroline sunk into the loving embrace of her new father, grateful for every moment in this new life.

The Sullivans, Millses, and Findleys were the only guests to see Daniel and Caroline wed. She had wanted it that way; there would be plenty of time over the coming years to share every other aspect of their lives with the neighbors, but now, in this most intimate moment, Caroline only wanted her nearest and dearest to witness. Hannah and her mother-in-law had spent much of the previous day cooking enough food for the dozen or so people, roping Abby in to help as much as they could manage.

Both the mayor and his wife were loath to let their daughter out of their sight. Though they didn't outright forbid her from speaking to Junior, Mrs. Mills seemed to never be farther than an arm's length away from the young couple.

Mercifully, the dozen or so wedding guests didn't stay long. Eating and toasting the newlyweds was exciting, but once the food was gone each person made his excuses, leaving Daniel and Caroline alone again.

After she waved goodbye to Hannah and Ben, Caroline turned to her husband. She was so happy she didn't think she could even speak, so she merely took a deep breath and held out her hand to him.

"You're home, my love," he whispered to her. "I will be by your side here every day. You never have to be without a roof over your head ever again."

Thank you so much for reading *Journey's End*, the first book of my spin-off series OREGON AT LAST.

If you read Caroline's first book—*Westward Courage*, book one of COURAGE ON THE OREGON TRAIL—then you know that the books in that series all end as the wagon company reaches the end of the trail. That was always intended to be the end of that story; the struggle to get from their comfortable homes in the east to their destination was the whole point.

But as I put out more and more of those books I started getting more and more emails and reviews asking what happens when the characters get to Oregon.

I have to admit I resisted writing this series for several years. There is just a lot less research easily available about this particular location in this particular time period. (If you happen to know of any good historical resources about the Oregon Territory in 1851, send them my way).

But now that it's started (four books out as of my

writing this author note), I am loving diving deep into it. I'm not sure when the series will come back around to Caroline and Daniel, but I feel sure that the hardest part of their journey is over.

One of my favorite parts of this book is actually Abby Mills—her independence and her being so utterly mistaken about what her mother wants from her. The mother-daughter dynamic (in real life and in books) is so complicated and layered. I had fun writing those two characters so deeply misunderstanding each other.

As we move forward in time, as the group of migrants settle in and build their houses and figure out how to eke out a living in this new territory, I hope you'll join me. There are so many more characters whose stories need to be told. We have a school to build and a first harvest to bring in and children to be born.

Thank you for reading this series, this book, and for getting this far. A review on your favorite retailer, or getting this book into the hands of a friend would be so appreciated.

A.T. Butler

September 13, 2023

this far demanded more of her than she had been prepared for.

As she settles in to her new home, Annie now faces her first Christmas without her oldest sister at the same time she has her first Christmas as a wife.

Will she be able to meet the expectations of her new husband, her new community, while still being true to herself as her sister would have wanted?

For all the stories of how these brave pioneers got to Oregon, look for the book series Courage on the Oregon Trail by A.T. Butler.

Grab _Christmas in Oregon_ here!
(on Kindle and Kindle Unlimited)

ALSO BY A.T. BUTLER

Courage On The Oregon Trail Series:

Westward Courage

Faithful Trail

Frontier Sisters

Unyielding Heart

Wild Promise

Fierce Dreams

Seeking Home

Trouble and Grace (2024)

Oregon At Last Series:

Journey's End

Christmas in Oregon

Snowbound Promises

The Pastor's Baby

Frontier Fortune

Reluctant Spring

Jacob Payne, Bounty Hunter Series:

Trouble By Any Name

Danger in the Canyon

Justice for Jasper

Blood on the Mountain

__Outlaw Country__

__Death By Grit__

__Desert Rage__

__Arizona Legend__

__Fool's Demise__

__Silent Night__

Bountiful Justice Series:

__Loyalty's Price__

__Riding for Justice__

__Trail of Redemption__

Other Western Novels by A.T. Butler:

__Hawke's Revenge__

ABOUT THE AUTHOR

I grew up in the southwest—California Missions, snakes and constant threat of drought weaving the backdrop of my childhood.

But it wasn't until I moved to Texas a few years ago that the magic and mythology of the American West began to seep into my soul.

I'd love to write about western adventures, strong women and noble men for a long time.

If you enjoyed this book, a review on your favorite retailer would be greatly appreciated.

- A